Ridin' for Him, Dyin' for Her

A Novel By CoCo J.

Text **LEOSULLIVAN** to **22828** to join our mailing list!

To submit a manuscript for our review, email us at
leosullivanpresents@gmail.com

© 2015
Published by Leo Sullivan Presents
www.leolsullivan.com

Acknowledgments

First off, I would like to give thanks to God. Because with out him, I wouldn't be who I am today.

Mommy-Kristie Fluker I love you baby. And I thank you for raising me to have respect and morals.

Maw-Maw-Linda Fluker-Garrison I love you so much. You're my world. Thank you for everything you've ever done for me.

My Auntie's and Uncle- Carolyn Whatley, Letha Fluker-Gill, Oretha Fluker and Wayne Fluker. I love y'all so much.

Nanny-Lanelle Whatley, I love you baby.

Lyneisha Logan, Jayla, Corey, and Maya Fluker. La'Jara and Ja'Marcus Whatley. I love y'all. And I'm proud to call myself y'all big sister.

My Favorite Guy- Terry, we've been through so much within these last four years. But it's all been worth it. I love you & our princess more than anything in this world. T.N.C for life.

All my cousins- It's too many of y'all too name this time around. I just want y'all to know,

I love y'all equally the same.

Kendra Littleton, Tammi C., Kiesha Wallace, Nikki Ervin, Mary Bishop and Ta'liyah Johnson. Thank Y'all for the support. I love y'all.

Best friend- Kiana Hall. I love you so much. You're always there when I need you.

My Fallen Angels

My paw-paw Wilmar (Chank) Garrison Jr., my great-grandfather, Logan Fluker. My great-grandmother Nellie Mae Jemison Fluker. My uncles, Logan Jr., Steven (you know I'm FOREVER Bout It' Bout It'), Desmond, Keyshawn, and Brandon Fluker, and James Whatley. My cousins Ike Burns and Keith Fluker. My god brother, Charles (Chuckie) Whatley. I love and miss each and every one of you. May y'all continue to watch over me, and continue to rest peacefully.

This book is dedicated to my one and only daughter Ni'elle Simone Williams. I love you baby girl, and everything I do from this point forward is for you. And my two god sons. Marc Jr. and Terence Jr. I love y'all both.

Special shout out to all the authors signed under Sullivan Publications. #WeAreFamily
My Fans-I haven't forgotten about y'all. Special thanks to each and everyone of y'all. I truly appreciate all the love and support y'all show me. Thank y'all!!!!!!

Chapter One
Ja'Mea

"You know what Ja'Mea, you honestly pissing me the fuck off. I swear you are!" my best friend, Taylor, all but yelled at me as I sat in her living room crying my eyes out. "You really just need to leave his ass alone, he don't fucking love yo ass like he say he do. No man is going to constantly keep putting his hands on a woman he loves. But never mind, I had to remember who I was talking about, Jermiah is not a man," she told me, and I really broke down crying. She was right, I needed to leave Jermiah's ass alone for good.

"I just don't know what to do. He's the only man I've ever been with," I cried.

"Mea, he's not a damn man, he's a little ass boy. Like I just told you, a man would never put his hands on a woman, I wish you would understand that shit. I'm not sitting here trying to fuss at you. I'm telling you this because I don't want him to go too far one day and he will kill you. Ja'Mea, tell me something, what happened to the girl I used to know? What happened to tuff ass Mea who didn't give a fuck about a nigga and would shoot his ass without hesitating?"

"I don't know Tay, his ass broke me, he really broke me," I told her as I thought about what's been going on between my boyfriend Jermiah and I.

Four hours earlier

"Jermiah, please no, don't do this!" I screamed, begging as his foot came down on my rib for the fourth time. I balled myself up in a fetal position and just took the hits. Tears fell down my face as he continued to kick and punch me like I was some nigga out on the streets that stole something from him.

"Bitch, the very next time I come home and tell yo ass to do something, if yo ass know like I know, you better fucking listen! Now get yo dumb ass up and clean up this fucking blood," he yelled as he spat in my face before finally walking out the bathroom.

When he left out the bathroom, instead of me getting up, I just laid there on the bathroom floor in a pool of my own blood, crying.

I was so sick and tired of Jermiah's ass coming home again drunk as all out doors, wanting to have sex with me. I denied his ass, and just like any other time I would deny his ass, he would beat me. I hated having sex with him while he was drunk. It turned me completely off.

I slowly got up from the floor with tears rapidly running down my face. I looked in the mirror at myself and cringed. My lip is swollen, and both of my eyes were turning black. This was starting to become a normal look for me. Anytime Jermiah's ass would come home drunk, or even when he had a problem going on in the streets, he would come home and take all of his frustrations out on me. I had become his personal punching bag.

Let me introduce myself, my name is Ja'Mea or Mea. I live in Augusta GA, with my crazy ass boyfriend, Jermiah. I'm only 18, while he's 22. I met him four years ago at a party that I was attending with my best friend Taylor, and since meeting him, we have always been together. He even had me move in with him six months after meeting.

During the first three years of us dating, he was the perfect man to me. He always catered to my wants and needs, and gave me any and everything I asked for, which wasn't much because I hardly ever asked him for anything. The only thing I really ever asked him was for time and loyalty. I couldn't even begin to tell you where things between us went wrong, but somewhere down the line it did.

I can still remember the first time he came home and beat my ass; it was a year ago. He came home drunk and mad as hell, because he had gotten his ass beat by some big time dope boys, and when I say they beat his ass, I mean they beat his ass until he was blue and black. When I tried to help him clean his wounds up, he pushed me down. I fell right down on my ass, looking up at him like he was crazy. After that, I really don't know what happened next because I blacked out.

When I woke up, I was in the shower with the cold water running down on my body. I got out the shower and looked into the mirror. I wanted to throw up, just looking at myself. I couldn't believe his ass would really put his hands on me. My face looked horrible, it was battered and bruised, I asked myself over and over again, how could Jermiah do this to me, how could he put his hands on me.

"Bitch didn't I tell yo ass to clean this fucking blood up? If the shit stain my fucking floor, I swear to god I'ma murk ya dumb ass," Jermiah said as he walked in the bathroom to take a piss. I looked under the sink and grabbed the cleaning supplies and started cleaning. "I'm about to dip, and when I get back yo ass better have my dinner on the table," he told me, walking out the bathroom. I knew damn well his ass most likely wasn't coming home tonight.

After I finished cleaning up the blood, I hopped in the shower so I could get the dried up blood that was on me off.

"Why am I still with him?" I asked myself as I let even more tears fall. I loved Jermiah with all my heart, but I knew he didn't love me the same. At one point, I think he did really love me, but over time; the love just faded away. Of course, I tried leaving his ass a few times, but he would always find me; and beat my ass, then he would tell me if I ever tried to do it again he

would kill me and my mama. Even though my mother was a no good drug addict, I still loved her with all my heart, and wouldn't want no harm to ever come to her because of me.

I stood in the shower until the water went from hot to cold. I got out and wrapped a towel around my body, and walked into the room. I applied my lotion I got from Victoria's Secret, and put on a red Adidas jogging suit, before putting on some red and white Adidas gym shoes. I grabbed my cell phone, and car keys, and walked out the door. I wasn't cooking Jermiah shit, I was leaving, and I damn sure was not gon' look back.

"Mea, please tell me you're going to just leave his ass for good. He's not the right person for you, and I'm sure you're going to find the man that is right for you," Taylor said with tears in her eyes.

"I am Tay, I'm really leaving. I can't continue to walk around with black eyes and a swollen lip," I told her as we both wiped our tears away. Right then and there, I made a promise to myself that was my last time crying over Jermiah Pickett's no good ass.

Three weeks later

After everything that went down with me and Jermiah, I've been staying at Taylor's house. There was no way in hell I was going back to Jermiah's house, and have him beat my ass again. My body was still healing from the last ass whooping he gave me three weeks ago.

I knew at some point I was gon' have to run into his ass, but I wasn't ready for that to be right now. That's why I didn't even bother going back to the house to get any of my things. He could burn everything for all I cared, I could buy more. Right now, I was just trying to focus on getting my life back on track. Less than a month ago, I graduated from high school with honors, and now, I was planning on attending Clark Atlanta University in the fall.

"Mea, are you up?" Taylor asked me as she knocked on my room door, before walking in.

Tay and I have been best friends since the womb; her mom and my mom were best friends well, they were best friends until my mom got with her husband, and he got her hooked on heroin.

Taylor is 5'2 and light skinned with long red hair, a big booty, and even bigger breasts. She had her dimples pierced and with the piercing, she looked just like Chyna.

"Ty'Shuan got some extra tickets to the Jeezy, Future, and Ciara concert tonight, do you want to go?" she asked me, referring to her boyfriend.

"Yeah, I don't see why not, I need something to do. I'm tired of sitting in this damn room with my mind on Jermiah's ass," I said as I sat all the way up in the bed.

"Yeah yo as really do, I'm tired of yo' ass just sitting up in this damn room looking like a damn sad puppy," she laughed as she walked out the door, closing it back behind her.

I got out the bed and walked over to the full length mirror in the room. I looked at myself and tears instantly fell down my face. I can't believe I let Jermiah break me all the way down like I wasn't shit. I let him treat me as if I was an ugly duckling. I let him walk all over me and everything. I damn sure wasn't ugly, I was brown-skinned, standing at only 4'8 with shoulder length light brown hair, hazel eyes, and braces. I didn't have a big booty like most girls from the South, but I was working with a lil' something, something back there, and my boobs were just average, they weren't little, and they weren't big. If you asked me, they were just right.

An hour later, both Tay and I were standing in her bathroom applying make-up. Neither one of us needed it, but because of my black eye, I had to apply some, and she wanted to put some on just because. I looked at myself and smiled; I was wearing a white off the shoulder crop top, some black booty shorts, and my Jordan 10's. Tay had on a skin-tight mini dress, showing off all her curves, and she had on some black spiked Red Bottoms.

"You know Shuan is gon' kick yo ass when he see that damn dress," I told Tay as we got into my 2013 Camaro.

"Girl please, that fool better leave me the hell alone, we are not together anymore, so that means I can do what I want, when I want," she said, getting into the car.

As soon as I closed my door, a text message came through; it was from none other than, Jermiah.

Jermiah: (7:24PM) "Bby, can u please cum back home?? I miss u it's been 3 weeks nd I been goin' crazy wit out u..-I promise u I wnt hurt u nomo" the text read. I didn't even text his ass back, I just stared at the message.

"Uh heffa, what the hell are you standing there crying about?" Tay asked. I hadn't even realize that I was crying until she said something about it.

"Jermiah texted me."

"Ja'Mea MiDora Wade. Yo ass better wipe them damn tears from yo face right now. We're supposed to be going out and having a good time, not thinking about that no good ass nigga! Put his ass on block and call it a day."

"I know, I know. I'm sorry," I told her as I wiped my tears away and turned the radio up.

****

When we got to Phillips Arena, it was packed as hell; we could barely find us a parking spot, but we were lucky enough to find one close to the entrance.

"Let me call Ty'Shuan's ass," Taylor pulled out her phone-, and I fixed my make-up. "Yeah stupid ass, we're outside, so meet us at the door," she told him, hanging up the phone before she began to apply some MAC lip gloss on her lips.

"Taylor why the fuck you got on that short ass dress man?" Shuan yelled at Tay as we walked towards the entrance, where he was standing with some man I've never seen before.

"Because I fucking can, and I thought I looked fine in it. Plus I came here to find me a new man," she smirked. I laughed at her ass; she knew all the right things to say and do to get under Shuan's skin.

"Yo on the real Tay, stop playing with me. You gon' make me catch a damn charge up in here tonight," Shuan told her as he pulled her closer to him.

I was feeling awkward as hell, because the man that was standing with Shuan was just staring at me like he had problem. He was fine as hell; he around 6'2 and brown-skinned with long curly hair that was in a ponytail. Just looking at his ass had me feeling some type of way.

"You got an eye problem or something?" I asked him, finally getting enough of him just staring at me and not say anything.

"Yo, you got a slick ass mouth ma."

"Okay and your point is?" I snapped.

"Ky, you better leave my damn best friend alone before we jump yo ass, then she shoot you."

"Come on na Tay, you know damn well I'm not worried about y'all. I stay strapped. But introduce me to ya friend."

"Mea, this is Ky irritating ass, Ky this my best friend Mea," Taylor said, giving me a smirk before nodding her head. I just rolled my eyes at her and looked back at Ky. Her ass was forever trying to play match maker.
"It's nice to meet you shorty," he said, but I didn't reply to his ass; I just turned around and waited until we could go sit down because my damn feet were killing me.

After the show, we all decided to go to the Jeezy after party at Royale's Palace, in Downtown Atlanta. Of course, all my ass wanted to do was go home and get some sleep because, I was tired as hell, but I knew I couldn't leave Tay out by herself even though I knew she was more than likely going to be going home after the club with Shuan.

"Tay, I'm going to the bar, I need a damn drink," I yelled in Tay's ear over the music as we stood on the dance floor dancing; she nodded her head, and I made my way towards the bar rapping along to Jeezy's *'Fuck the World'*.

> *I said she never been to college, got brains*
> *And one thing about it, IQ is insane*
> *My G' gon' keep it up, she ain't gon' let it be*
> *Then once she get it started, it might not never end*
> *Hit her on the late night, tell her that I'm 'bout to fall through*
> *Said it's been waitin' on you nigga, get us all you*
> *She got a little paper, might just tell her "let me hold some"*
> *I said I'm on my way, you just go ahead and roll one*
> *She said just come through, and I'ma roll*

a few
And make it stand tall, then I'ma roll on
you
If she was Bonnie, I be Clyde, we been
down since way back
Swear them lips illegal, they addictive like
crack
That's what I told her.

I was still rapping along until I felt somebody grab on my arm. I turned around ready to cuss whoever the hell it was out, that was until I saw the devil himself. Jermiah.

"Bitch I been calling and texting you for the longest! Is this why you couldn't answer the phone bitch? You out here being a ho'!" he yelled as he pulled me closer, "bitch I should beat the fuck outta yo ass."

"Jermiah, let me the fuck go!" I tried snatching my arm away from his crazy ass, but he had a damn death grip on it.

"Shut the fuck up ho' and bring yo ass on," he told me as he walked towards the exit, basically dragging my ass along with him.

When we got outside of the club, people were standing around but they were all drunk and so into their own world that they hadn't realized I was being forced against my will to go with this crazy fool.

"Jermiah, please, just let me go!" I cried as he slammed me against a car and grabbed me around my neck, choking the hell out of me.

"Bitch, yo ass thought you could just get up and leave me? You outta yo motherfucking mind? I should kill ya dumb ass right here and now, but I got something else in store for you," he said as spit flew from him mouth with every word he said.

"Jermiah…please, just let me go," I got out as he tighten his grip around my neck, making it even harder for me to breath. This nigga was trying to kill me for sure.

"Nigga, if I heard her correct, I could have sworn she said let her the fuck go," I heard a voice from behind Jermiah say.

"Nigga this don't have shit do with yo ass. This shit right here is between me and this dumb bitch," Jermiah replied, not even turning around to see who he was talking too.

"Nigga let her the fuck go before I empty this clip in ya bitch ass!" Ky said, taking his gun off safety and putting it up to Jermiah's head. He let my neck go, and I fell to the ground coughing, "yo, you ight ma?" Ky asked, looking down at me. I nodded my head, and he turned his attention back to Jermiah. "Nigga, if I ever catch yo ass around here again, I can promise you I'ma blow ya fucking brains out."

"You got that fam," Jermiah told him as he looked down at me and smirked, before walking away.

"You sure you straight?" Ky asked as he bent down.

"Yes, I'm fine, thank you." I mumbled. I knew as long as Jermiah was still alive, he would never leave me alone.

"Don't worry ma, he ain't gon' be fucking with you ever again, I'ma make sure of that," he told me, and it was like he was reading my mind.

Chapter Two
Kyrie

"Ky, I know yo ass hear me talking to you!" my baby mama Shayreese said to me as she snapped her hand in my face.

"Yó Reese, back the hell up man, and what the hell I tell you about putting yo hands in my fucking face?"

"Then answer my fucking question. Are you coming to get your damn kids tomorrow, or do you want to drop them off at your momma's house?" she was asking, but I wasn't paying no attention to her ass. I was looking at how that bitch nigga Miah was man handling shorty that was with Tay earlier, and pulling her out the club.

I'm the type of nigga not to get into other people's business, but when I saw her Miah was man handling her, then I walked outside and saw how he had her choked up on a car, I almost lost my cool and killed that nigga right then and there, but I didn't. I let his ass walk away with his life.

"Come on ma, get on up off the ground," I held my hand out to her, and she grabbed it as I helped her up off the ground.

"Kyrie, who the fuck is this bitch?" I heard from behind me, I turned around and Shayreese was standing there with her hands on her hips.

"Shay, if you don't get the fuck away from me with all that bullshit you're talking," I turned back around to face Mea; she was standing there looking at me with one of her eyebrows raised.

"Nigga, I was fucking talking to you, and yo ass just up and walked away from me before answering me to talk to this bitch?" Shayreese was now standing directly behind me; I shook my head because I knew how her ghetto ass could get.

"Look, Shay man go back in the club. I'll holla at you tomorrow," I said to her, turning around and giving her a *don't fuck with me right now* look. "You sure you're okay?" I asked, turning back around to face Mea, but before she could answer me, Tay spoke from behind me.

"There you go, I was looking all over for yo ass. What the hell are y'all out here doing?" I turned back around, and she and Shuan were walking towards us.

"What's going on man?" I questioned, noticing people were now walking out the club behind them.

"They started fighting, you know how people start to acting when they get drunk. Mea, are you okay?" Tay shook her head as she walked over to her friend.

"Yeah, I'm good, just ready to go home and get in my bed, that's all."

"Before you go home and get in the bed, let's go get something to eat. I don't know about y'all, but I'm hungry than a motherfucker," Shuan said as he pulled Tay into his arms.

"No nigga, you drunk and high, let me go," she mushed his head.

"On the real, I am hungry, so y'all down or what?"

"It's whatever."

"I don't know," Mea said; I looked at her and she was looking all sad and shit.

"Come on Mea, you know you're hungry, let's just go get something to eat, then we can go home," Tay replied. It took Mea a few minutes, but she finally agreed to go.

We ended up going to Hooters on Peachtree; mostly everybody that was at the club also ended up there before they headed home, so you know the place was crowded.

"So ma, tell me something about ya self," I said to Ja'Mea as she took a sip of the cold drink.

"I mean, there's not much to tell. I'm 18, just graduated from high school a few weeks ago, and I plan on attending Clark Atlanta in the fall, that's about it."

"So what's going on with you and that fuck nigga Miah? You fuck with his ass or something?"

"I used to date him, but I left him a few weeks ago," she mumbled so low that I barely heard her. I nodded my head; no wonder why that nigga was handling her like that, his ass was mad she left him.

"So since you don't fuck with his ass no more, can I take you out sometime?"

"No thank you," she straight shot my ass down.

"Damn Ky, I didn't believe it when I heard bitches was walking around calling you ugly, but shit I guess it's true," Shuan laughed, I couldn't lie, getting turned down by Mea had me feeling some type of way.

I wasn't a desperate nigga by far, but it was just something about lil' ma that had me wanting to get to know her, wanting her period.

"Tay, can we please go?" Mea asked as she looked up from her phone.

"Aye lil' ma, let me see ya phone."

"For what?" she snapped, I didn't even bother to answer her. I yanked the phone from her hand and looked down at it, and on the screen was a text message from that fuck nigga Miah.

Jermiah: (1:59AM) "U think dat nigga gne keep u safe bitch?? I can't wait 2 get my hands on ur ass"

Me: (2:03AM) "don't worry nigga.. I'm gon' always be around to keep her safe, now fuck wit her if u want!" I texted back. I knew I should have just killed his ass right then and there instead of letting him walk away, that's what I get for being nice to a fuck boy like him.

"Yo lil' ma, I'ma take you home tonight," I told her as I gave her back her phone, only after putting Miah's number on the block list.

"No thank you, I'm good, besides I'm

driving my own car."

"I don't think that was a question, I was telling you I was taking you home tonight, and don't worry about yo car it's gon' be good," I told her, getting up and waiting for her to get up, but she just stayed seated with a frown on her face. Even when she was frowning, she was still beautiful.

"Mea, let him take you, I'ma go home with Ty'Shuan. He's too drunk to be driving himself home," Tay told her. A few seconds later, she got up and shook her head. I knew she was mad, but I was just doing this to help her out.

****

"Lil ma' get up, we're here." I shook Mea so she could wake up.

"Where are we? This ain't Tay's house."

"This my crib, we're in Druid Hills. Come on lil' ma, get out," I told her as I got out the car before she could reply or say something smart like I knew she wanted to. I walked to the porch before turning around; Mea was still sitting in the car with her arms folded across her chest, "look lil' ma, if you don't get out the car then I'ma have to come get you out if it. But one way or another, you are getting out the car," I said, unlocking the door. When I walked in the house, I heard the car door open and close.

"Why am I here?" she snapped as she walked in the house.

"Lil' ma, on some real shit, you can lose the damn attitude, you lucky I brung yo ass to my crib anyway, especially since I don't know you. But to answer your question, I brung you here because Tay is going to Shuan's house, and that fuck nigga Miah probably know where she stays," I said as I walked up the stairs with her following behind me. "You can sleep in here, and I'll be downstairs if you need me," I told her as I grabbed her a pair of my basketball shorts and a white t-shirt. "There's some towels and stuff already in the bathroom," I told her before walking out the bedroom.

The next morning I woke up and sat up, trying to figure out why was I sleeping in one of the guests bedrooms, instead of my own. Just then, I remembered that Mea was upstairs sleeping in mine. I got up and walked up the stairs to see if she was up. When I got closer to the door, I could hear sniffles coming from the room. I knocked on the door once before walking in. Mea was sitting up in the bed crying, but she hurried and tried to wipe the tears away when I walked in.

"What's wrong lil' ma?"

"Nothing,"

"Something wrong with you sitting up in here crying and shit."

"It's nothing."

"If you say so, but if you wanna talk, just let me know, I'm here," I replied as I walked into my closet to get me something to wear so I could get in the shower.

When I got out the shower, Mea was still sitting up in the bed, but this time she was watching TV and looking down at her phone. I grabbed my phone from the dresser and noticed I had a few missed calls, and they all were from Shayreese. I dialed her back as I walked out the room, and down the stairs.

"So you so busy over there fucking some bitch that you couldn't even answer the damn phone for me? What if it was a damn emergency?" Shay yelled in my damn ear, having me pull the phone away from my ear.

"Shay, if you dlon't lower your fucking tone when you're talking to me, I'ma hurt ya ass. And don't worry about who I'm fucking 'cause it ain't yo ass," I told her sitting, down on the sofa.

"What the fuck ever Kyrie, when are you coming to get these bad ass kids."

"What the fuck is so important that you want me to come get my kids this damn early?

"None of your damn business, now are you gon' come get them, or do you want me to drop them off?"

"You know damn well I ain't telling yo rat ass where I stay. I'll be there in a hour." I hung up the phone, put it down on the table. I didn't regret having my kids because they were the best things that ever happened to me, but they mama was a bitter bitch.

I got up from the sofa and walked in the kitchen to grab me a bottle of water, before going upstairs.

"Yo lil' ma, get up and get in the shower. I'ma take you to get some clothes, then we gon' go get something to eat." She didn't say anything, she just got out the bed, and walked into the bathroom.

I took Mea to Tay's house so she could get her some more clothes, before driving to Reese's apartment a few minutes away. I swear, I hated the fact that Shay ass was staying in these damn apartments with my kids. I wanted them to stay with me at my crib, but every time I mentioned it to Shay's ass, she would threaten me with the police, and in my line of work, I didn't need the boys on my ass.

When I pulled up, Shay was sitting outside with her Thot ass friends Trice and Siara,

"I'll be right back," I told Mea as I got out the car and walked right past them.

"What? Yo ass don't know how to speak now?" I heard Shay speak from behind me, but I ignored her and continued to walk into her apartment. When I got in there, it was a damn mess. Toys and clothes, along with trash was everywhere. My five year old triplets Kyrie Jr., Kylan, and Kyria all were sitting on the sofa watching TV.

"What's up daddy babies," I said to them; they all looked at me, hopped off the sofa, and ran over to where I was standing.

"Hey Daddy!" they all yelled unison. I hugged them, then turned around to look at Shay's trifling ass.

"Why the fuck this apartment looking like this?"

"Because they don't know how to clean up behind themselves, and who the fuck is that bitch you brought over here?"

"Don't worry about who she is," I rolled my eyes and turned towards my babies.

"Daddy, can we come with you?" Kyria asked me.

"Of course y'all can, go in the room and get your bags."

"Ky, I don't want kids around that unknown ass bitch," she told me as she got up in my face., I shook my head, ignoring her ass as I waited for my kids.

Two minutes later, they walked back in the living room with their book bags and walked over to me.

"Y'all ready?"

They nodded their heads, and I picked up Kyria, and grabbed Kylan and Kyrie Jr.'s hands before walking out the door.

"Ky, I'm not fucking playing with yo ass. You better drop that bitch off where she belong! If I find out she was around my fucking kids, I'm gon' raise hell!" Shay yelled as I put the kids in the car.

"Y'all put y'all seatbelts on," I closed the door, and walked to the driver's side. "Mea, these are my babies Kyrie Jr., Kylan, and Kyria." Ja'Mea turned around in her seat and waved at them; they all waved back at her, except for Kyria.

"Hi, I'm Kyria. You're pretty, are you my daddy's girlfriend?" she smiled

"Hi Kyria, thank you. You're pretty also. And no. I'm just your daddy's friend," Mea said as I chuckled.

I took everyone to Roscoe's House of Chicken & Waffles. Kyria was talking Mea's head off, while Kyrie Jr and Kylan just sat there being quiet. They barely even touched the food that was sitting in front of them, and that wasn't like them. I made a mental note to see what was going on with them, when we got back to my house.

After eating, I took them to the park so they could play. I knew they damn momma hadn't took them to the park, or let them do anything fun; they were only allowed to sit in front of the apartment building, and play with the other kids out there.

"Your kids are beautiful," Mea told me as she came and sat down next to me.

"Thank you, I see my baby girl has taken a liking to you," I nodded my head towards Kyria, who was running towards us.

"Yeah she has," Mea smiled.

"Come on Mea, come push me on the swings again," Kyria giggled as she grabbed her hand and dragged her towards the swings.

I watched as Mea went from pushing Kyria, to pushing Kylan, to pushing Kyrie Jr. on the swings, I was glad they were having fun. I was still watching them when my phone vibrated in my pocket. I took it out and I had a text message.

Siara: "r u still comin 2 see me 2night?"

Me: Na ma, I don't think I am. I got some business to handle."

Just as I sat my phone down on the table I

was sitting on, it rung. I looked at the screen, and it was my nigga Shuan.

"Yo, what's good my nigga?" I answered

"Yo, where yo ass at?"

"Shit, park with Mea and my kids, why? What's the word?"

"Nothing right now, just put Taylor ass to sleep," he laughed, "I just might go make some rounds and pop up on niggas, see how them candy shops looking," he said, talking in code.

"I don't even know if I'm gon' make my rounds tonight, but if I don't, send Dez to handle that for me."

"Ight my nigga. I'ma holla and let you know what's going."

"Fasho," I said, hanging up the phone and walking towards Ja'Mea and my Tre'.

"Are y'all ready to go?" I asked them, and of course they all shook they head no, "Too bad, y'all don't have another choice," I laughed as I helped Mea get them off the swings.

"Lil' ma do you wanna go home or back to my house?" I asked Mea before pulling off.

"I think I'll go back to your house, Tay is still with Shuan," she said, and nodded my head.

When we got back to my house, I ordered some pizza; we were going to have a family movie night. Mea was in my room helping Kyria in the tub, while I was helping Kylan and Kyrie Jr.

"Kylan, Kyria Jr, what's going on with y'all? Tell daddy what's wrong?" I asked them when I noticed how they didn't want to take they clothes off. They looked at each other before looking back at me. "Tell me what's going on." They shook they heads no. "Y'all get in the tub, I'll be right back," I told them, walking out the bathroom. I walked down the hall to my room, and I walked in the bathroom where Kyria was sitting in the tub, playing with some toys while Mea sat on the toilet seat.

"Kyria baby girl, what's going on with your brothers? Why won't they take their shirts off?"

"Cause mommy and her boyfriends be hitting them, they have marks and stuff. Mommy told them don't tell you or she was gon' do it again," Kyria said as she went back to playing with her toys. I was heated as hell when she told me that shit. I don't even put my hands on   .

females, but I was gon' beat the living hell outta her ass.

I went back in the bathroom where the boys were taking a bath, and they were in the tub with their shirts on.

"Take them shirts off right now," I told them with bass in my voice. They did what I said and I turned each of them around. When I saw all the bruises my sons had on their backs, all I saw was red, fuck beating that bitch

Chapter Three
Taylor

"Ty'Shuan, I promise you this. If you don't answer your fucking phone, I'ma shoot ya dick off and staple it to ya damn forehead," I said on Ty'Shuan's voicemail before hanging up, then going to my call log. I dialed Mea's number and waited for her to pick up.

"Hey bestie, what's up? What you doing?" she answered on the second ring.

"Girl nothing, waiting to see if Ty'Shuan ass call me back within ten minutes before all hell breaks loose, where you at?"

"I'm still over Ky's house."

"Hmp, you've been over there for a few weeks. Y'all are getting pretty close huh?" I laughed. I was happy my best friend wasn't sitting at home in her room, stuck on Jermiah's lying no good ass.

"Yeah, I guess you can say that, but I hardly ever see his ass. I've been over her with his kids."

"His ass always running the streets huh? I

know the feeling, and aw, he let you meet his kids? That must really mean he likes yo ass."

"So wait, why are you waiting on Shuan to call you back?" she asked, and I knew she was changing the subject on purpose.

"So I can snap on his ass."

"Oh lawd, what he done did now?"

"His ass out there cheating on me, and think he slicks," I shook my head; I can't believe I was going through this shit.

"How do you know he's cheating? And who do you think it's with?"

"Because some bitch tagged him in a status on Facebook, the shit came to my phone, but when I got on there it wasn't up no more. I guess he told the bitch to take it down. I don't know who the bitch is, but what I do know is I'm about to ride through the hood and see if I see his ass out there. He got me fucked up on all types of levels," I told her, and she laughed.

"Oh goodness, well I'm riding with yo crazy ass."

"Okay, meet me at my house," I told her, hanging up the phone and going into the bathroom.

Twenty minutes later, Mea and I were pulling up at my house in Buckhead at the same time.

"Girl, when was the last time yo ass been home?" she asked me as she got in my car.

"Shit the day of the concert," I laughed.

"So yo ass was just gon' forget all about me huh?"

"Nah boo, I can never forget about my best friend. I knew you were still over Ky's house. If you would have told me you were coming home, best believe I would have been here with you," I told her, pulling off.

We were driving through Decatur, and because it was damn near 100 degrees outside, everybody and they mama's was outside.

"Look, there he go right there," Mea said as she pointed over to the Ridgewood apartments. I looked over to where she pointed and instantly got pissed off. Yeah, this nigga really had me fucked up.

Ty'Shuan was sitting on his 2015 all black Magnum, with some bitch standing in between his legs, smiling all in his face.

"So this the type of shit you out here

doing?" I asked him, getting out my car.

"Aw shit," I heard Ky say. I looked over at his ass and he was standing there hugged up with a bitch. I looked at Mea, and could tell she was mad, but I also know she wasn't gon' say nothing to him.

"Tay, what yo ass doing out here man?" Ty'Shuan's dumb ass had the nerve to ask me. I was really trying my hardest not to beat his ass out here.

"Nigga don't fucking ask me what I'm doing out here, I should be asking yo dumb ass what the fuck you doing out here? Is this what you call working? Having some bitch all up in yo face?"

"Who the fuck yo rat ass calling a bitch, bitch?" the lil' ho' he was flirting with asked me, like I wouldn't hesitate to pop the bitch in her mouth.

"I do believe I was talking to you bitch."

"The only bitch I see around here is you, ho'."

"Aye Shanice, chill out with all that bullshit right there. Tay, let me holla at you for a minute," he told me as he grabbed my arm and walked me away from everybody else. "Go home Taylor, I'll be there in a few, man."

"Go home for what? So you can fuck this low life ho' then come home to me? Nah playa, you got the game all fucked up, but it's good, let that ho' know he can have you, I'm done," I told him as I yanked my arm away from him and walked towards my car.

"Shuan you need to keep yo ho's in check," I heard the lil' bitch say. See I was gon' leave calmly, but all that shit went out the window when that bitch opened her mouth. I turned around and walked back towards the bitch and before she knew what happened, I had her ass on the ground, and I was on top of her, punching her in her face.

"SHUAN, GET THIS CRAZY HO' OFF ME NOW!" she screamed as I hit her in her eyes, mouth, and nose.

"Come on Tay, get off the girl, you done enough," I heard Ty'Shuan say as he picked me up off the bitch.

"Let me the fuck go!" I told Shuan as I started fighting his ass; he had me all types of fucked up, just like that bitch. "I swear I'm so done with yo lying cheating ass!" I screamed as he put me down. I punched his ass in the face one more time before looking around for Mea, only to notice she was fighting the bitch Ky was all hugged up with.

I laughed at Ky, because he was struggling to get Mea off the girl, so I walked over to help him out, although I should have just let her keep fighting the bitch, but I knew she would just end up killing the poor girl.

"Come on Mea-Mea, that's enough," I said as Ky finally grabbed her away from the girl. She yanked away from him and walked towards my car. I shook my head at him before walking away and getting into my car.

"Come here Taylor,"

"Fuck you nigga." I got into my car.

"Yeah okay, yo ass better be at my house when I get there."

I stuck my middle finger up, and pulled off.

"We going out tonight, and I don't even wanna hear no for a answer," I told Mea.

If yo dude come close to me
He gon' wanna ride off in the ghost with

me (I'll make him do it)
I might let your boy chauffeur me
But he gotta eat the booty like groceries
But he gotta get rid of these hoes for me
I might have that nigga sailing his soul for
me
Ooh, that's how it post to be
If he wants me to expose the freak
Ooh, that's how it post to be
Ooh, that's how it post to be
Oh, that's how it post to be
Everything good like it post to be

Mea and I sang along with the song, as we danced on the dance floor. I was dancing my ass off when I felt somebody grab me from behind. I turned around and a tall dude that looked like Fabulous, only he was light-skinned, was standing behind me as I grinded my hips. I smiled before turning around to continue dancing.

I danced with Fab Jr for four songs straight, before I got hot and needed to get me something to drink. Mea and Fab Jr walked with me.

"Can I get you anything?" the bartender

asked in an annoyed voice. I was about to snap on her ass before Mea touched my arm; she knew me so well.

"Two shots of Ciroc," Mea told her, as I mugged her daffy duck looking ass. The bitch lucky I ain't feel like getting put out the club tonight, or I would jumped across the bar and beat her ass.

"So ma, can I get your number, I wanna take you out somewhere after the club," Fab Jr told me.

"Nigga what you can get is the fuck up outta her face before I give you some hot led," Ty'Shuan said from behind me. I turned around and he was standing there with Ky, Dez, Charlie, and Toby, and they all stood there mugging me and Fab Jr. I laughed because Ty'Shuan had some fucking nerves.

"Yo Shuan, I ain't know this was yo girl, my bad man."

"I don't belong to him, I'm a single woman and can do what the hell I wanna do, and talk to who the hell I wanna talk to."

"Mea, can I talk to you for a second?" Ky asked Ja'Mea; I looked at her and she was downing another shot.

"No."

"Nigga, what you still standing here for?"
Ty'Shuan asked Fab Jr.; of course the nigga
didn't say anything, he just walked away. I shook
my head before walking back on the dance floor.

I was back dancing and grinding my hips
when somebody else came up behind me and
grabbed my hips just as *'Fetty Wap's My Way'*
came on.

Baby won't you come my way?
Got something I want to say
Cannot keep you on my brain
But first I'ma start by saying this, ayy
All headshots if you think you can take my
bitch, ayy
And I'm too turnt, when I shoot, I swear I
won't miss, ayy
Ba-Baby won't you come my way?
Baby won't you come my way?

I danced on him, until I heard a gun cock
behind me; I turned around and Ty'Shuan's
crazy ass was standing there holding a gun to the
nigga head.

"Nigga like Fetty say, 'all headshots if you

think you can take my bitch, and best believe I don't miss. Now you got five seconds to get yo motherfucking hands off her before I lay yo ass out in this bitch!"

The dude turned around and tried to punch Ty'Shuan, but Ty'Shuan stepped back and hit the nigga in the head with the butt of his gun, before shooting him in his leg. Hearing the gun shot, all hell broke loose in the club; everybody was running wild. I felt somebody grab on to my arm and looked to see it was Mea.

"Come on man, we gotta get the fuck outta here," Ky yelled to us. We all followed him towards the back entrance.

"TAYLOR, TAKE YO ASS HOME RIGHT FUCKING NOW, AND DON'T STOP NO FUCKING WHERE, AND I MEAN THAT SHIT!" Ty'Shuan screamed at me as me and Mea ran to my car.

We pulled up to my house at the same as Ty'Shuan and Ky, and both of them was looking pissed, but I ain't give not one fuck! All that shit happened because of Ty'Shuan, so the only person his ass should have been mad at was his damn self. I got out the car and walked into the house with Ty'Shuan calling my name. I tried closing the door in his face, but he pushed it open.

"Bring yo ass here right fucking now!"

"Get the fuck outta my house." I walked towards the back of my house.

"Come here Taylor Faye," Ty'Shuan said as he followed behind me. I didn't know why this nigga was following me, he better take his ass to one of his ho's house. I kept walking to my room, but before I could make it to the door, he grabbed my arm and turned me around to face him.

"Ty'Shuan, let me go and get the hell out!" I struggled to get away from him.

"Come on ma, let me explain myself."

"Ain't shit to explain man, yo ass cheated, point blank. I called and texted yo ass at least ten times that day before I popped up on yo ass, and you was so busy entertaining some bitches that you couldn't even answer for me? The shit could have been a fucking emergency," I yelled, trying to get my hands loose so I could smack fire from his ass.

"CALM THE FUCK DOWN TAYLOR!"

50

he yelled; I couldn't lie, that shit turned me completely on.

"Fuck you, let me go, and get the fuck outta here."

"I'ma let you go, but Tay, I promise yo ass, if you hit me again I'ma really fuck yo ass up," he told me; he let my arms go and I pushed past him and into my room.

When I got in my room, I stripped until I was in my panties and bra, and I turned around and Ty'Shuan was just standing there looking at me, licking his lip.

"What you don't understand English or something? Get out, I'm done with yo cheating ass," I spat as I walked into the bathroom and started the shower.

"You can never be done with me," he told me as he took his clothes off as I stepped into the shower.

"Ty'Shuan, I am not about to play these lil' games with you," I said as he got into the shower and pushed me against the wall, grabbing between my legs.

He inserted a finger inside my love box, and I let out a moan.

"You still want me to stop?" he asked as he viciously fingered fucked me.

"Huh, answer me Taylor, do you want me to stop?" He was still finger fucking me, as he trailed kisses from my neck and down the middle of my body, until he was face to face with my pussy. He lifted my leg up and placed it on his shoulder as he dove in head first and started eating me out.

"Shiiittt Ty'Shuan, that feels so good baby." He stopped what he was doing and stood up.

"What the hell you think you doing?" I snapped.

"You told me to stop, remember?" he laughed, but I didn't see shit funny.

"You right, let me go call my boo from the club and have him finish it," I replied, trying to get out the shower.

Before I had one foot out the shower, Ty'Shuan grabbed me by my hair and pulled me back in.

"Why the fuck you keep playing with me like I'ma fuck boy Taylor?" he grilled me as he grabbed my hands and pinned them above my head; his ass must have known I was about to beat his ass. Again.

"I'm not playing with you, and I won't ever play with yo ass again. Tell one of them nasty ho's you fucking with to play with you," I spat as he forcefully turned me around.

"Bend that ass over and touch them toes," he said as he roughly grabbed my neck and made me bend over himself. I smiled, because this is just what I wanted.

He entered me roughly in one swift motion, and I couldn't lie, that shit hurt, but I was gon' suck it up and take it like a champ. He grabbed my hips as I started throwing my ass back, matching him thrust for thrust.

"Yeah, that's right ma, throw that shit back, throw that ass back for daddy," Ty'Shuan said as he smacked me on my left ass cheek, before smacking the right.

"Shiiittt, Ty'Shuannn, right there baby. Don't stop!" I yelled as he was hitting my spot. I swear, that shit was feeling so good.

"You about to make it rain for daddy?"

"Yesssss, I'm aboutttt too cummmm!"

"Cum for daddy then, and daddy gon' cum

with you!" he growled as he started pumping in me at the same time as I felt myself explode all over his dick.

"Aahhhh!" I yelled out as I felt him release his seeds inside of me. For about three minutes, we stayed just like that so we could catch our breath.

After we actually showered, I didn't say shit to him;, I was still pissed at his ass, and I wasn't just gon' give in just like that because he put the dick game down on me. He had me fucked up. I stepped out the shower, dried myself off, then put on my panties and bra before getting in my bed.

I pulled the cover over my head, just as Ty'Shuan walked in with nothing but his boxers on.

"Look ma, I'm sorry, I know I fucked up. But can you please forgive me? I need you in my life ma. I love you," he told me as he walked over to the bed and pulled the covers off my face. I had tears in my eyes, but wiped them away quickly.

"Come on ma, don't be in here crying. I really am sorry." He got in the bed with me and pulled me closer to him.

"I hate you, I really do," I whispered as I cried into his chest. I can't believe how loving Ty'Shuan made me a weak bitch.

"I love you too ma," he said, kissing the top of my head.

Chapter Four
Ja'Mea

It's been almost two months since I last saw Kyrie the night Shuan shot that nigga in the club. I can't even front, I felt some type of way of me not talking to him, and I was still a little mad that I saw him hugged up with some bitch. Deep down I knew that I shouldn't really be mad; he wasn't my man and I wasn't his girl. The only reason I beat the bitch ass, was because she thought she was about to jump in that fight with Tay and the bitch she was fighting, but she had another thing coming. I wore her ass out, and if I was to ever see her ass again, I was more than likely going to do it again.

Since seeing Kyrie at the club, he's been calling and texting me, but I had yet to answer any of the calls, or text him back. I didn't have time for him, I was just trying to focus on starting school. I was majoring in Journalism and minoring in Communication, plus I was also starting my new job working at Roscoe's Chicken & Waffles. I was also trying to get some new stuff for when I move into my new condo Tay and I rented in Downtown Atlanta. I had a few dollars saved up from when I was with Jermiah; every time he would give me some money, I would take half of it and go shopping, and the other half I would put up for a rainy day.

"Mea, Ky is here to see you," I heard Tay say from the other side of the door as I tried to arrange my room just the way I liked it. I looked down at my clothes and saw I looked a hot mess. I was wearing some holey sweat pants with a sports bra, and my hair was all over my head. I worked a double shift last night because one of the workers called off at the last minute. I wasn't complaining though, that was more money for me, but I was tired ass hell. I put the shirt that was in my hand on top of one of the dressers in the room, and threw my nappy hair in a ponytail before walking out the room.

Ky was sitting on the sofa watching Sports Center, and drinking a Gatorade.

"What are you doing here?" I asked him, putting my hand on my hip and putting all my weight on the left side of my body.

"I wanna talk to you."

"I don't think we have anything to talk about."

"Yo what's your problem Ja'Mea?" he questioned me as he got up and walked over to me. I folded my arms across my chest and looked up at him; good gawd, this man was fine.

"I don't have a problem Kyrie, I just don't have time for anything right now. I'm getting ready to start school, plus I'm working." I walked away from him and sat down on the sofa. The smell of his Gucci cologne was doing something to me.

"So in between you getting ready to start school and working, you couldn't find the time to text me back? Or answer your phone?" I didn't even answer him, I picked up the remote, and started flipping through the channels.

"Seriously Ja'Mea?" He stood in front of the TV like his ass was made outta glass.

"I don't think neither one of your parents are made of glass, can you please move from in front the TV?" He shook his head before walking out the door, slamming it behind him. I got up and went back to my room.

Three hours later, I was finally done

rearranging my furniture in my room when my phone rung, I looked at the screen, and it was my mother's number. I hadn't talked to her since my freshman year of high school, and the last conversation we had, was her telling me to get out of her house.

"Hello," I answered, even though everything in me wanted to ignore the call.

"Hey baby girl, how are you?"

"I'm fine." As much as I wanted to hate my mama, I couldn't; something in me just wouldn't allow me to hate her.

"I need to talk to you about something important, can you please come over here?" I looked at the time, and saw that it was only 2 in the afternoon.

"Uh, yeah. I'll be over there a lil' later," I told her, hanging up the phone before she could say anything else. I got up from my bed and dialed Taylor's number since she had left for work thirty minutes ago.

"What's going on bestie?" she answered on the second ring.

"Can you talk? I gotta ride somewhere."

"Of course, you know I'm not doing

anything here," she laughed.

Taylor was an assistant manager at Wal-Mart, and of course her crazy ass don't do no type of work, but boss other workers around.

"So where you going to anyway?"

"See my mama, she just called me and told me she had something important to tell me, and asked me to come over."

"Before you head over there, ask yourself if you really want to go."

"Trust me, I did, and I'm sure. I just want you to stay on the phone with me while I drive there."

"You know I will."

"Alright, I'll call you back in about a hour, I gotta get in the shower."

"Okay," she said as we hung up the phone.

An hour later, I was dressed and ready to go, I had on a PINK joggin' suit with my Air Jordan 7's. I pulled my hair into a bushy pony tail, grabbed my keys, and walked out the door. As soon as I started my car up, I called Taylor back.

"Now, I'm gon' ask you one more time, are you sure you want to go see her? You know I won't judge you if yo say no," she answered.

"Yes I wanna go Taylor," I laughed.

"Alright."

Taylor and I talked about any and everything under the sun until I got to Dawson, I was nervous as hell. It'd been four years since I last saw my mama, and the memories of when she put me out her house with nowhere to go was still fresh on my mind.

Four Years Ago

"Ja'Mea MiDora Wade. Bring yo ass down these motherfucking steps right fucking now!" my mom yelled. I put down my school book before getting up to go see what my mama wanted now.

"Yes?"

"Don't fucking 'yes' me, what the hell is this bullshit?" she asked, holding up an empty condom wrapper.

"I don't know ma, ask yo no good ass husband what it is," I rolled my eyes and turned around, only to find her good for nothing husband, Seth sitting on the sofa smirking at me.

"I did ask him, he told me it came from your room! So, you're having boys in my house?"

"Bullshit, he did not get that shit from my room."

"I don't fucking believe you, are you having sex?"

"No!" I all but yelled. I couldn't believe my mama would believe her husband over here own daughter, but then again, when it came to Seth's ass, he could do no wrong in her eyes.

SMACK!

"Bitch don't you ever raise your voice at me, and don't ever in yo life lie to me."

"I'm not having sex mama, Seth is lying,"

"She the one that's lying, she's having sex with her drug dealing boyfriend, everybody knows it too."

"He's lying mama!" I cried, *SMACK!* She smacked me again.

"You know what, get the fuck outta my house, and don't bring yo ass back ho'. I don't ever wanna see you again!" she yelled at me before pushing me down. I got up from the floor and went back up stairs. I grabbed stuff I knew I

really needed and walked out the door, without
even looking back.

For a few months I stayed with Taylor and
her family, until Jermiah insisted I move in with
him, and that was the worst mistake I could ever
make in my life.

"Mea, did you hear what I said?" Taylor
asked me as I pulled up in front of my mom's
house.

"Huh, what did you say?"

"I asked were you okay? I heard sniffling,
are you crying?"

"No, but I'm here, I'll call you later." I
hung up the phone before she could say anything
else. I got out the car and walked towards the
door. I knocked twice before I heard my mama
yell for me to come in.

As soon as I walked in the door, I wanted
to walk right back out. The house was a damn
mess. Trash was everywhere, and my mama and
her no good ass husband Seth were sitting on the
sofa smoking on a cigarette.
"I didn't know he would still be here," I said as I
walked all the way in the house, and close the
door.

"Don't come in here being disrespectful!" Seth said as he smiled at me.

"Seth, can you please give me and Mea a few minutes so we can talk?" my mama asked; Seth looked at her and nodded his head before getting up and walking past me, all the while licking his lips. That shit creeped me the hell out.

"Have a seat baby girl," she told me when Seth walked up the stairs.

"No thank you, I'll stand."

"Suit yourself, so I saw in the papers that you just graduated with honors. That's good, how come you didn't you invite me to your graduation?" she asked with an attitude. Did this bitch really just ask me that bullshit?

"You wanted me to invite you to my graduation? Ma, the last time I talked to you, you made it perfectly clear that you didn't want to see me again, so there was no way I was gon' come over here and invite you to my damn graduation, there was no way in hell you were going to ruin the happiest day in my life by downing me and calling me all kinds of bitches and ho's."

"Watch your damn mouth when you're talking to me MiDora," she said, calling me by my middle name. "I am still your mother!"

"NOW YOU WANT TO BE MY
MOTHER? WHERE WAS MY MOTHER
FOUR YEARS AGO? YOU LET A FUCKING
MAN TELL YOU LIES ABOUT ME,
INSTEAD OF YOU BELIEVING ME AND
WHAT I TOLD YOU, WHICH WAS THE
TRUTH, YOU BELIEVE A FUCKING MAN
OVER YOUR CHILD! YO FLESH AND
BLOOD, THEN YOU PUT ME OUT TO FEND
FOR MYSELF. I DON'T HAVE A MOTHER!"
I screamed, with tears rolling down my face.

"Ja'M-" she started, but I held up my hand.

"Save that shit, I don't even know why I
came over here,-" I said, turning around to leave,
only to be face to face with Seth.

He was standing there with a sadistic smile
on his face.

"Seth, get the hell out of my way," I tried
pushing past him, but he grabbed my arm and
pushed me down on the floor. I quickly hopped
up. I didn't know what the hell was on the floor.
"Please get out my way.-"

"You're not going nowhere until I get
what I want," he told me, licking his lips.

"Mea, just let him get off, it's going to be over soon!" my mother said; I turned around to look at her ass like she was crazy.

"Bitch are you outta yo fucking mind?" I asked her.

I turned back around and tried to fight past Seth, but his ass was strong. He slapped me across the face before kneeing me in my stomach. I doubled over in pain, then fell to my knees. While I was on my knees, Seth kneed me in my face and I fell back on the ground. He quickly got on top of me and started pulling his pants down.

"Seth, please don't do this! Please, I'll give you some money, name your price!" I cried.

He had his pants down and he was working on pulling my pants down. I was still trying to fight him when I felt my mama grab my hands and tie them to the coffee table that we were next to.

"Mama, please don't let him do this to me!" I cried; I couldn't believe this shit was happening to me. What did I do to deserve this?

"Shut the fuck up bitch!" Seth said, punching me in my mouth as he ripped my underwear off and forced himself into me with so much force that I blacked up.

When I woke up, I knew instantly by the beeping noises and the smell I was in a hospital. I sat up and tried to remember what happened, then it all started flooding back, and I felt myself hyperventilating.

"Mea, are you okay?" I heard Taylor ask as nurses rushed in the room.

"Miss. Wade, calm down. You're going to be fine," an elderly one said as she stood next to me while I cried. Taylor walked into my view and grabbed my hand.

"It's okay Mea, everything is okay," she told me.

"Where am I? What hospital am I at?"

"Putney Memorial, what happened Mea? Who did this to you?" she asked me, just as a few police officers walked in the room.

"Hi Miss. Wade, I know you probably don't feel like answering any questions, but it's mandatory we ask them. Do you know who did this to?"

I shook my head, "No, whoever it was had a mask on they face," I lied; I wasn't telling the police shit, I was gon' handle this shit myself.

"What were you doing there?"

"That's my old home, I was supposed to be meeting my mother there, but she never showed up,"

"So you don't remember anything?" I shook my head no again, "Okay, if you do remember anything just come down to the station," the officer said before walking out the door. The nurse was still in there checking my vitals.

"What happened Mea? Who did this to you?" Tay asked me as soon as the nurse left out the room.

"How did you know I was still there?" I asked her ignoring her question.

"I was calling you back to back, and you never answered the phone. I started getting worried, so I tracked your phone and saw you was still at your mama's house, I called Ty'Shuan and told him to come ride with me."

"Where is he now?"

"He went to get something to eat with Ky."

"Wait, Ky is here?"

"Yeah, he's the one that found you, whoever did this to you dragged you to the kitchen and hid you under the table," she said, shaking her head.

"Seth did this," I mumbled as Ky and Shuan walked in the room.

"Yo shorty, you straight?" Shaun asked me as he sat down in the other chair in the room, next to Tay. Ky just stood by the door looking at me like I had something on my forehead.

"Mea, I know I didn't hear you right, I know you didn't just say Seth did this shit to you?" Tay spat out before I could answer Shaun.

"Who is Seth?"

"Her mother's husband."

"I don't have a mother, that bitch is dead to me!" I angrily said.

"Mea, what happened baby?" Tay asked, getting up from her chair, and sitting down on the bed next to me.

"When I got there, Janice and Seth were sitting down on the sofa smoking a cigarette, I told Janice that I didn't know Seth would still be there. He said I was being disrespectful and before we could started arguing, my mom asked

Seth to leave us alone so we could talk."

"Seth walked up the stairs and my mom asked why she didn't get an invitation to my graduation, and I basically told her she didn't deserve to be at my graduation. I told her ass off and tried to leave, and when I turned around Seth was standing there. He slapped me in my face, then he kneed me in my stomach, before kneeing me in my mouth. I tried to fight him off, but my mama tied my hands to the table an-" I couldn't go on anymore. I just broke down.

"It's going to be okay Mea," Taylor said as she pulled me to her and I leaned my head on her shoulder.

I was released from the hospital the next day, and I just wanted to go home and lock myself in my room. I didn't want to talk to anybody, nor did I want to see anybody. Taylor called my job and let them know what was going on, and they told her they were going to hire a temporary employee until I was ready to come back, I was fine with that. Every day Tay, Ky and Shaun made it their mission to come check on me, and each day I would tell them I was okay, and I didn't need them to come check on me, but deep down inside I wasn't okay how could my mother do this to? How could she just stand there while her husband raped me? How could she not stop him? I asked myself those questions every day when I thought about what happened to me.

Chapter Five
Kyrie

It's been a few weeks since that shit happened with Mea. I couldn't lie, seeing her all battered and bruised the way she was had me all fucked up in the head. On top of me worrying about her, I had shit going on in the streets. First one of my workers came up missing. A few days after he came up missing, his body parts was sent to his mom's house cut up. Then somebody hit one of my houses. I guess the saying *'when it rains it pours'* was most definitely true, because it sure as hell was pouring down on my ass right now. I still had niggas out looking for Shayreese ass. After I got my babies from her house, she dipped and haven't even been back, but I promise to God, when I find that bitch I'ma make her ass suffer.

"Daddy, I wanna go see Mea, I haven't seen her in a billion trillion days," Kyria said as she walked into the living room, where I was sitting, watching ESPN.

"She's sick right now baby girl, and she

don't want to see anybody right now. Where are your brothers?"

"She do wanna see me, I know she do, I can make her feel better, I'll make her a card and make her some soup. And they're playing outside on the swing."

"Alright, well go ahead and make her the card, then we'll make the soup together, then we'll bring it to her."

I could never tell Kyria no, hell I couldn't tell Kyrie Jr or Kylan no either. They always got what they wanted from me, no matter what it was. Kyria hopped off the sofa and skipped out the living room, heading towards the back door.

Three hours later, I was pulling up to Ja'Mea and Taylor's condo with Kyria, Kyrie Jr, and Kylan. Each of them made her a card and we all made the soup. Before I could get out the car, my business phone rung, I took it out my pocket and saw it was my nigga Dez calling.

"Dez, boy what's the word?"

"Shit man, I was just calling to see if you was rollin' through that lil' party at the strip club tonight?"

"You talking about Kay shit?"

"Yeah, you know she said this her last time performing."

"That bitch been saying that for the last two year now," I said as we both laughed. "But I don't know bro, I might roll through. But look, let me hit you back, I got something to handle," I told him as I looked back at the kids and Kyria was giving me the evil eye. I couldn't do nothing but laugh at her ass.

"Ight," he said as we hung up the phone.

"Alright, come on y'all," I said, getting out the car before I opened the door for them.

I used the extra key Tay gave to Shuan and unlocked the door.

"Y'all stay right here, I'll be right back," I told my Tre' before walking up towards Ja'Mea's room. I knocked twice before just walking in, and she was sitting up in her bed with her Kindle in her hand. She looked good as hell with her hair in a high pony tail and her reading glasses on.

"What are you doing here?" she asked, looking up at me for a few seconds before looking back down at her Kindle.

"I got a surprise for you, come in the living

room."

"No thank you,"

"Come on Mea, you been sitting in this bed for too long, get up lil' ma," I said, walking towards the bed. I took a good look at her face, and her eyes were puffy and she had bags under them. "When was the last time you slept?"

"Mea, I know my daddy told you I was out there," I heard Kyria say from behind me. I turned around and she was standing in the door way with her hands on her hips looking up at Ja'Mea.

"Kyria didn't I tell yo lil' self to stay out there?"

"Yeah you did, but you was taking too long. I wanted to see my Mea," she said as she walked over to the bed and climbed on it. "I miss you Mea, daddy said you was sick and didn't want to see nobody. Not even me, but I told him that wasn't true, you wanted to see me. Me Kyrie Jr and Kylan made you some cards and some soup. Come on, let's go in the living room," Kyria told her.

"Okay, but let me go clean myself up. I'll be out there," Ja'Mea said, getting out the bed, and walking towards the bathroom.

Thirty minutes later, Ja'Mea walked into the living room with some basketball shorts and a wife beater on. Her hair was no longer in ponytail, it was now wet and curly, hanging down her back; she still had her glasses on.

"Hey Mea," Kylan said as he got off the sofa and hugged her.

"Hey Kylan, you missed me too?"

"Yeah."

"What about you Kyrie Jr? You didn't miss me?"

"I did," Kyrie Jr. said, getting up to hug her too.

"Alright y'all that's enough. It's my turn," Kyria said as she got off the sofa and walked over to Ja'Mea. Kyria held her hands out and Ja'Mea picked her up.

"Where is the soup and cards y'all made me?"

Three hours later, my Tre' were in Ja'Mea's bed sleeping, and Ja'Mea and I was sitting on the sofa watching her favorite movie, *Shottas*.

"Thank you," she mumbled; I looked over

at her, and she was looking over at me.

"What are you thanking me for?"

"For bringing the kids over here, I don't know why, but seeing Kyria really helped me out. Especially her smart ass mouth," she said as she laughed.

"Yeah she do have a smart mouth. But I'm glad they came over here, I needed to see you smiling again."

"So what are your plans for the night?"

"I gotta handle some business," I lied, well I really didn't lie. I did need to handle some business, but I was also gon' slide through Onyx tonight.

"You taking the kids to their mother house?"

"Hell no, my babies not going back over there, I was gon' take them to either my mama or sister house."

"I'll watch them, Tay is working a double shift and she won't be home until tomorrow morning."

"Are you sure you're up for it?"

"Yes."

"Alright, well I'll drop y'all off at my

house, you cool with that?" she nodded her head, and smiled.

Two hours later, I helped Ja'Mea give the kids a bath and let them watch a movie, before they all fell asleep in my bed, including Ja'Mea. I took one quick picture of them, leaving out the house.

> *It really hurt when they killed Shotty*
> *I was locked down in my cell and I had to read about it*
> *And when they killed Diddy, left him out in Philly*
> *We was young and gettin' money, man we use to run the city*
> *We was rockin' all them shows, fuckin' all them hoes*
> *And when they killed Darryl, Renee had to see him froze on the ground*
> *Downtown, I can hear the sounds now*
> *When she walked up to the casket, seen her son and fell down*
> *I drop tears for my niggas that ain't here*
> *And still think about you even though that it been years*
> *Cause half the niggas I grew up with is all*

dead
All this pain and all this stressin' I should
have a bald head
Cause when my aunt Rhonda died, she
looked Tock in his eyes
Saw death comin', when she seen it she
just cried
Prolly part of the reason we drink and we
get high
When I find the nigga that killed my daddy,
know I'ma ride
Hope you hear me, I'ma kill you nigga
To let you know that I don't feel you nigga
Yeah, you ripped my family apart and
made my momma cry
So when I see you nigga, it's gon' be a
homicide
Cuz I was only a toddler, you left me
traumatized
You made me man of the house, and it was
gridin' time
So I'ma let this flame hit you just to let this
pain hit you
And for all them cloudy days, I'ma let this
rain hit you nigga

I know, I know, I know, I know
I know, I know, I know, I know
You ripped my family apart and made my
momma cry
So when I see you nigga it's gon' be a
homicide
I know, I know, I know, I know
I know, I know, I know, I know
So I'ma let this flame hit you, just to let
this pain hit you
And for all them cloudy days I'ma let this
rain hit you nigga

Meek Mill's *Traumatized* played as I drove, checking up on my traps. Just listening to the lyrics of the song had me thinking back to when my pops got killed.

My dad, Kyson, was the biggest drug dealer in Atlanta and the surrounding areas; hell, you might as well say the whole state of Georgia. Every time you looked around, somebody had his product, but you know how the game go. Niggas don't like seeing another motherfucker happy.

It was the day of my sister's 10th birthday, and we were going shopping to get her some clothes for her party. I was only 5 at the time. My dad stopped at a gas station, and I watched how every nigga that passed him up spoke to him and showed him admiration. I knew right then and there, I wanted to be like pops when I grew up.

My pops was coming from inside the gas station when about three or four niggas walked up to him, surrounding him. My mother saw what was going on, so she locked the car doors and told me and my sister Kyla to get down on the floor. A few seconds later, we heard gun shots; my head instantly popped up as I watched my dad fall to the ground, holding his chest.

"Dadddy!" Kyla screamed out as they fired some more shots in my pops body. I got a good look at them niggas faces; I can't believe they asses were dumb enough not to wear any masks, but I made a promise I was gon' make them niggas feel the pain me, my mom, and sister went through.

I was snapped out my thoughts by my phone ringing.

"What's good?"

"Yooo, where you at foolio?" Shuan asked from the other end of the phone.

"Shit, just riding past the candy shops.

About to head to Onyx, where you at?"

"Pulling up at Onyx."

"Ight, I'll be there soon my dawg," I told him, hanging up the phone.

When I got to Onyx, that bitch was packed. Kay knew how to throw her a goodbye party. Shit her ass had one every four months. I looked over to the V.I.P section where Shuan, Dez, Charlie and Toby all were sitting in there getting lap dances; I couldn't do nothing but laugh at them niggas. They loved spending they money on these stripper ho's.

"My nigga, I ain't even think yo ass was gon' show up," Shuan slurred; I knew that nigga was drunk. I was gon' have to drop his ass off at the crib before I headed home.

"What's good with y'all niggas? Y'all in here getting white boy wasted?" I asked them as all the light shut off. Instead of people getting frantic, everyone shut the fuck up. I found me a seat in the dark and sat down. As soon as I sat down, the lights on the stage came on.

"*Introducing the main attraction tonight, Special K!*" The DJ yelled into his mic as Ciara's 'Body Party begin to play and Kay's fine ass slid down the pole from the roof. I just shook my head; her ass was always doing some other shit just to get these niggas for they money, and they all fell for it, but I respected shorty she was all about her money.

"Yo Ky ain't that yo baby momma over there?" Toby asked me, nodding towards the bar in the V.I.P section. I looked over to the bar, and sure enough that bitch Shay was dressed in a strippers outfit and was shaking her ass for some nigga sitting at the bar. I stood up and made sure I had my pistol with me before walking towards the bitch.

I grabbed her ass by her hair, and dragged her over to the corner.-"Bitch you was putting yo hands on my fucking sons?" I asked as she looked up at me like she saw a damn ghost.

"Yo fam, let my bitch go before I air this bitch out!" some nigga from behind me said. I turned around to a familiar face. I knew his ass from somewhere, but I just didn't know from where, but I knew eventually it would come to me.

This nigga had the game fucked up if he thought he was about to step to me in this bitch.

"Derrick, just leave it alone, he's my baby's father," Shay said from behind me; I turned around to face her ass. I took one look at her rat ass and hauled off and smacked her ass. I hit her so hard she fell on the ground. I swear I wasn't the type of nigga to put my hands on a female, but this bitch had it coming.

As soon as I turned around that bitch nigga swung on me, but his ass was a lil' to slow for me. I stepped back then threw a punch that connected to his jaw; his mouth was instantly leaking. Some nigga hit me in the back of my head with a bottle, and the next thing I know, there was an all-out brawl in that bitch.

****

"Yo, who the fuck was that nigga?" Shuan asked me as Dez drove me home from the hospital. After security broke that shit up, my head was leaking and I had to get some stitches, plus I had a damn concussion.

"I don't know even know man, but what I do know is I saw his ass before. I just can't place him," I said, shaking my head. I was really trying to remember where I saw that nigga before.

"So that's Shay new nigga?"

"I guess so, bruh, I'm telling you, when I see that bitch I'ma murk her dumb ass.

When Dez pulled up to my crib, I dapped him up, and he let me know he was gon' bring my car by sometime tomorrow. I nodded my head and got out the car. When I got in the house, Ja'Mea and my Tre' all were asleep in my bed. I went into the bathroom to get in the shower so I could join them. My damn head was killing me.

Over the next few weeks I had been trying to get in touch with Shay ass, but she had been M.I.A; her ass wasn't even working at the strip club no more. She still hadn't showed back up to her house, and none of her rat ass friends saw her either. I wanted to know who that one nigga she was with so bad that I had Dez go to Onyx and grab the video tape from the club. I had him, Charlie, Toby and even Shuan look at it to see if they recognized the nigga, but they didn't, so I had Charlie do a face recognition to see who he was. I was just waiting on the results.

Chapter Six
Ty'Shuan

"This some straight up bullshit!" I yelled as I paced the floor of Arneisha's living room, "I can't believe this shit man!"

"Well it's not some bullshit, and you better believe it!" she snapped; if this bitch knew like I knew, she would just shut the fuck up right now.

"Look bitch, this shit right here is your fucking fault. I might lose my fucking girl because of this shit."

"That ain't my fucking fault. I ain't tell yo no good ass to cheat on her and get me pregnant," she said. I was trying my hardest not to smack the living soul outta this bitch right now.

"Bitch it is yo fucking fault. Yo ho' ass told me you was on fucking birth control when we started fucking."

"So just because I told you I was on birth control you thought that was an okay sign for you to go in me raw? News flash nigga, being on birth control isn't always effective," she told me,

"I don't have time for this shit, I'm going take a nap."

I sat down on the sofa and picked up the piece of paper that was sitting on the table, it was the DNA test I had ordered. When I got the first set of results, I didn't believe them, so I had four more tests done and they all said the same thing.

I was stuck as hell; how could I tell Taylor that I got a bitch pregnant and that she was almost 8 months pregnant? The same bitch she caught me with. If she didn't kill me, I knew she was gon' leave my ass for sure. I sighed before getting up and walking out the door, slamming it behind me. Instead of me going home, where I knew Taylor was waiting on me, I was just gon' ride around and try to clear my mind, I couldn't face Taylor right now, I just couldn't.

Just as I was getting in my car, I got a text from Ky.

Ky: (3:17PM) meet me at the candy shop in Bankhead," the text read, and I started my car and pulled right off.

When I got to our trap house in Bankhead, Ky, Charlie, Toby and Dez all were standing outside in front of Ky's car.

"What's good my niggas?" I asked them, getting out of my car and walking towards them.

"Shit man, just tryna figure out what the hell going on."

"What you mean?"

"That nigga young B' called and told me some lil' nigga was trying to rob the Buckhead trap, but Brandon walked up just in time. He bringing the nigga over here now."

"You got beef with some niggas out here?" I asked him.

"Shit not that I know off, except maybe Miah and that one nigga from the club the other week. Speaking of that. Still no results?"

"The only information I got on his ass was his first name, and that's Derrick. Everything else isn't local. So I have to do a world wide check, and that's gon' take some time," he replied as Brandon pulled up, and it didn't look like he had anybody in her car.

"Where that nigga at?" Ky asked, walking over to Brandon's car.
"Jack is bringing him around back in the van, we knew people were going to be outside," he told us. I looked around and knew they did the right

thing.

We all walked into the house just as Jack and Rell were bringing dude body in the house.

"Bring his ass in the basement, niggas handling business up here,." Ky said told them.

When we got in the basement, Jack and Rell already had the nigga tied down to one of the chairs that was down there. I took a seat, and so did Toby, Charlie, and Dez. Kyrie was standing in front of the lil' nigga and Jack, Brandon, and Rell all were standing behind him.

"Alright lil' nigga, we can do this the easy way, or we can do this the hard way. Now I'ma only ask you this one time, and one time only. Who the fuck sent you?" Kyrie asked as he leaned down until he was face to face with the lil' nigga.

"Nigga, I ain't telling y'all shit. What y'all think I'ma snitch? Y'all got me fucked up. Y'all might as well kill me!"

"Ight, yo wish is my command," Kyrie told him taking his 9 from his waist band and sending four hot ones in the nigga dome. "Take a picture of this nigga and find out who he is, then bring his body to his momma house," Kyrie told

Brandon, Rell and Jack, they nodded they heads, and Kyrie walked up the stairs with me following behind him.

"Yo, you straight my nigga?" I asked him once we got outside.

"Nah man, I need a drink bad. You wanna slide through Onyx with me?"

"Fasho, you know I'm down."

When we got to Onyx, even though it was the middle of the day, I looked over at Ky as we started walking towards our section and noticed he was looking around. I knew he was looking for his rat ass baby momma, but he might as well stop looking for her, that ho' was nowhere to be found. I knew he put a bounty on her head, but no one was supposed to kill her; they were only to bring her in alive. I guess she got wind of the bounty and got the fuck on.

"Yo Shuan, I heard Arneisha pregnant by you, yo girl know?" Siara asked me as she and her sister Trice walked over to where Ky and myself was sitting.

"Man if y'all ho's don't get the fuck from over here with all that bullshit," Ky said as he flagged a waitress.

"What's good Shuan, Ky. What can I get y'all?" Scandalous asked.

"Nah ma, send somebody else over here," Ky told her ass. Shit I wouldn't have wanted to order a drink from her ass either. Her name wasn't Scandalous for nothing. If you looked up the word Scandalous in the dictionary, there would be a picture of her ass.

"Whatever," she said, rolling her eyes and walking away.

"Yo, what the fuck y'all two bitches still standing here for? Get the fuck on!" Ky told Siara and Trice; they didn't say anything. All they did was roll their eyes and walked away.

Two hours later, Ky and I both were buzzed as hell. I knew neither one of us were able to drive ourselves home. I pulled out my phone to call Taylor; she had been texting me all day, and I ignored every single one of the text messages. I already knew when she answered the phone she was gon' be on 10.

"What the fuck you want?" she snapped.

"Yooo, we need a ride."

"Who is we? And why the hell do y'all need a ride.

"Me and Ky, and because, we're drunk."

"Well call whatever bitch you was with earlier,"

"Come on Tay, I was handling business, I wasn't with no bitch. Just come get us. Why you sitting here playing man? You know damn well if either one of us try to drive and we get into a car accident and die, or even go to jail yo ass gon' feel bad."

"I'm on my way," she said, hanging up the phone.

"What her ass say?" Ky asked.

"Her usual bullshit, but she's on the way," I told him as he took another sip from the Henny bottle he was drinking on.

When Taylor walked, I knew it was gon' be some shit when she bumped into Siara and Trice. I got up, and tried to make it over to them before they started fighting, but I didn't make it quick enough. Both Trice and Siara were jumping Taylor, but Tay still had the upper hand on both of them ho's.

"I know one motherfucking thing, if y'all don't get the fuck on I'ma murk y'all dumb asses!"

"I swear on my momma, when I see y'all ho's again I'm beating y'all asses!" Taylor yelled at them as I carried her ass out the club. "Put me down Ty'Shuan."

"Tay, calm down baby," I told her as I put her down; she was trying to get back in the club.

"No, fuck that. Them bitches got me fucked up, move out my fucking way."

"Tay, I'm not gon' move. Just come home, let's go home." I told her as I grabbed her face and made her look into my eyes. She seemed to calm down and turned back around, walking to her car with me and Ky following behind her.

Instead of Taylor dropping either one of us off at our cribs, she took us back to her and Mea's condo. I knew she was still mad, and I had to sober up quick before we got into her room; I knew her crazy ass was gon' try to fight me too.

"You fucking one of them bitches Ty'Shuan, and please don't fucking lie to me!" she yelled as I walked into her room, closing the door behind me.

"What? No Taylor, I'm not messing with none of them ho's. Why the fuck are you always accusing me of cheating?"

"So tell me this, when was the last time you saw that rat bitch Arneisha?" she asked, ignoring my damn question.

"What? What that bitch gotta do with anything?"

"Just answer the question Ty'Shuan, when was the last time you saw her?" I swear Taylor was tripping right now.

I ignored her ass and sat down on the bed. I began taking off my shoes, then my shirt. As I was trying to get my shirt over my head, her crazy ass started swinging on me; I swear this bitch was crazy as hell.

"Taylor! Stop fucking hitting me I'm not playing with yo motherfucking ass!" I lightly pushed her ass off me and stood up. I looked at her ass, and she was like a lion ready to pounce on my ass again.

"Ty'Shuan, when was the last time you saw the bitch?" she asked in the calmest voice ever yeah this bitch was certified crazy.

"Taylor, I don't know. I don't know when the last time was."

"So you wasn't with her today?" she asked, putting her hands on her hips.

"No man, I was handling some business with Ky then we went to Onyx."

She didn't reply, she just walked over to her bed and grabbed her phone. She did something on there, then tossed to me. When I saw what was on the screen, I wanted to kill Nene's dumb ass. The dumb bitched posted the results of the pregnancy test on my wall, then tagged Taylor in it.

Arneisha Johnson- Nigga u thought u could just deny my baby??? U got the game fucked up! Ur child will be here in a few weeks. U mite as well tell ur bitch 2 get ready to be a step mommy. @Taylor Howard look ur nigga gt a baby on the way, and it's not by you"

I swear, I was gon' kill this bitch.

"So you got a baby on the way? You fucked this bitch raw Ty'Shuan?" Taylor asked me with so much hurt in her voice., I looked up at her and she had tears falling down her eyes. I got up, and tried to walk towards her, but she just stepped back, shaking her head.

"I'm sorry baby,"

"Please just leave me alone Ty'Shuan, I can't even look at you right now," she told me, walking out her room door. I put my shirt and shoes back on and walked behind her out the door. I was gon' give her some time to calm down, but in the mean time I had to go handle this bitch Nene.

****

When I got to Arneisha's house them rat bitches Siara and Trice both were sitting on the sofa looking down at their phones.

"Y'all two ho's get the fuck out, and I'm not gon' repeat myself," I told them in a deadly voice. They grabbed their belongings and practically ran out the front door.

"What the hell is wrong with yo ass?" Arneisha asked, walking back into the living room.

I closed the distance between us, and wrapped my hand around her fucking neck.

"Bitch what the fuck is your problem? Why the fuck would you do that shit? You one stupid bitch, I swear soon as I my seed get here, I'm taking her from yo unfit ass, then killing you!" I said as I tightened my grip, then let her ass go. I turned around and walked out the door.

Chapter Seven
Taylor

I couldn't believe this nigga Ty'Shuan would do this bullshit to me. After everything we've been through, he would do this to me. He would get some bitch pregnant. I swear when I saw that post I wanted to kill his ass, but I just kept my cool and walked away from his ass. I was officially done this time; I refused to sit around and let this nigga play me like a fucking fool. He knew me better than that.

"What's wrong?" Mea asked me, as she walked into the condo with her school books, and smelling just like chicken.

"Nothing, this damn work is stressing me out, plus I just found out I'm thirteen weeks pregnant," I said as the tears fell down my face.

"Oh my God, when did you find out?"

"I went to the doctor's today, but I'm not sure if I'm going to be keeping it," I told her as I put my head down.

"What? Why not Taylor?"

"Ja'Mea, now is not the time for me to be

bringing a child in this word. I'm a full time student, and I'm full time at both Wal-Marts, I really can't handle a baby right now," I told her, getting up and walking towards my room.

I know some people might call me selfish, but I was far from that. I just knew bringing a baby into the world wasn't the best thing for me or Ty'Shuan.

The next morning, Ja'Mea was driving me home from the clinic. She didn't agree with my decision to abort the baby, but she was there for me when I needed her the most.

"Are you gon' tell him about the abortion?" she asked me.

"No." She didn't say anything after that, she just nodded her head.

Ty'Shuan's ass been calling me non stop for the past three days, and I ignored every single one of his calls, even put his ass on the block list. Of course his ass even went as far as to call me from other numbers. I changed my number altogether. I had nothing to say to his ass, and he didn't have shit to say to me.

****

I was walking out of Wal-Mart, towards my car when I saw Ty'Shuan leaning on my car. I stopped walking for a minute, rolling my eyes and sighing, before I continued walking.

"So yo ass couldn't answer the fucking phone Taylor?" he asked me.

"We don't have shit to talk about, and get away from my car Ty'Shuan!"

"Taylor, why did you kill my baby?" he asked with so much hurt in his voice. I looked at his ass with narrow eyes before looking at the ground.

"Ty'Shuan, I can't talk about this right now. Please move out the way. I worked a double shift, and I need to get some sleep, I'm tired."

"I don't give a fuck about all that shit right now, Taylor. You mad because another bitch pregnant by me, that you go do some foul shit like that?" he asked, balling up his fist and walking to stand in my face.

"How do you even know about the abortion?"

"Don't fucking worry about how I know,

and no Mea didn't tell me! I just wanna know why you did it."

I sighed as tears ran down my face. "Ty'Shuan, please move out the way." He looked at me for a few seconds before moving out the way and walking towards his car. Although I'm still very much hurt by all the pain he caused me, I was still hurt because of the look he gave me. I got in my car and cried my eyes out before finally pulling off and heading to school.

I was so happy to be off for the next four days from both of my jobs, along with no having classes for the next week. This break is well needed, and I was gon' enjoy it to the fullest, because working two jobs every day and going to classes every other day is really starting to take a toll on me.

"Are you okay?" Mea asked me as she walked into the condo with books in one hand, and a cup of coffee in another.

"Yeah, I was just thinking. You plan on being up all night? I don't remember you drinking coffee before," I laughed.

"Yeah, three of my finals are in the same day, and I really need to study. Oh and Ky and

Shuan are about to come over," she told me as she sat the books down on the coffee table.

The last time I saw Ty'Shuan was when he came up to my job and confronted me about the abortion. I tried to call him once to apologize, but he didn't answer the phone. So I left him alone. Just as I got up to go to my room before he walked in the door, but I was too late. Both he and Ky walked in the room, each of them had a box of pizza in their hands.

"What's up Tay?" Ky asked me Ty'Shuan just sat on the sofa looking at his phone.

"Hey Ky, where yo bad ass kids at?"

"Chill out on my babies, but they with my momma for the weekend," he chuckled.

I was just getting out the shower, and walking into my room when Ty'Shuan walked in. He didn't say anything, he just sat down on the bed and put his head and in his hands. I walked over to him and lifted his head up, and made him look at me.

"I'm sorry Ty'Shuan, I know I should have told you I was pregnant, but even if I would have told you, that wouldn't have stopped me from getting the abortion."

"Tay, did you get the abortion because Arneisha's pregnant by me?"

"What no? I got the abortion because I'm working two jobs and going to school. I'm just not ready to have a baby yet." He didn't say anything, he just nodded his head and laid back on the bed. I climbed on the bed and straddled him. "I really am sorry Ty'Shuan, no matter how bad you hurt me, I would never do something like that to intentionally hurt you," I told him as I kissed his lips.

He grabbed the back of my head and kissed me back intensely; he stuck his tongue inside my mouth and palmed my ass.

"I missed you Tay, please forgive me for fucking with that bitch and getting her pregnant," he told me as he looked me in my eye; I didn't reply to him, I just went back to kissing him. He rolled me over, and he was now on top of me, I had my legs wrapped around his waist as he took his shirt off.

"You missed me?" I didn't say anything, I just nodded my head as he took his belt off, then pulled his pants down. Before he could get them all the way down his phone rung; he pulled it out his pocket, and sighed before answering it.

"What the fuck you want? What? What hospital? Ight I'm on my way," he told whoever it was in the phone as he hopped of the bed, putting his pants back on. I sat up in the bed and looked at him.

"What's going on?"

"Arneisha is going into labor," he told me. "I know you not feeling it, but can you please come up there with me? I need the support," he said, putting back on his shirt and looking at me. I just nodded my head.

****

Ky and Mea rode with me to Piedmont Hospital; Mea knew I was gon' need the support more than Ty'Shuan's ass. I was so happy I had a best friend like that.

"You straight Tay-Tay?" Ky asked me as we walked through the front doors of the hospital. I nodded my head, and he walked over to the Nurse's station. "They're on the 2nd floor," he told us, walking towards the elevator.

Me: (6:28) "We're in the waiting room."

My Baby: (6:29) "Ight, she's already pushin' I'll be out there soon"

"She's pushing," I told Ky and Mea.

"Are you sure you're okay?" Ja'Mea asked me as she came sat down next to me.

"I don't know, I don't know how I'm supposed to feel right now."

"Do you still love him?" I didn't say anything, I just nodded my head. Everything in me wanted to shake my head no, but I would be lying to not only Mea, but myself.

"She had twins, a girl and a boy. Ty'Nessa Monet' and Ty'Shuan Tyson Jr.," Ty'Shuan said with a somber look on his face.

"Shuan, what's wrong man?" Ky asked before I could.

"They're taking Ty'Shuan Jr. to run some test on him," he said in a low voice, sitting down next to me and putting his head in his hands.

"Did the doctor's say if anything was wrong with him?" Mea asked him; he didn't say anything, he just shook his head no.

"He has pneumonia and abscesses of the skin," Ty'Shuan said with tears in his eyes. I walked over to him, and hugged him.

"Is your daughter okay?"

"Yeah, she's straight. The doctors are still running more tests on Ty'Shuan Jr, though. But come on, let's go home. I can't take it here right now."

Chapter Eight
Ty'Shuan

I was stressing bad as hell; I felt like I was on the verge of losing my damn mind. My baby boy was still laid up in the hospital, and there wasn't shit I could do for him, it hurt me bad as hell to see him hooked up to all them tubes. He still had pneumonia, but they were saying something else caused the pneumonia, so they were still running some tests. Ty'Nessa was released a week ago, and she was at her momma's house, although I was planning on taking my babies away from Arneisha's unfit ass.

The day she and Ty'Nessa were discharged from the hospital, I went against my better judgment and let the bitch take her home, when I got to her house the bitch was sitting on the bed smoking weed, with my daughter laying right next to her. It really took everything in me not to beat her fucking ass. I did smack the bitch up a few times, and let her know that once my son was released from the hospital, he would be coming home with me, along with Ty'Nessa and

I dared that bitch to tell me something different.

Heart beatin' fast, let a nigga know that he alive

Fake niggas mad, snakes
Snakes in the grass, let a nigga know that he arrive
Don't be sleepin' on your level cause it's beauty in the struggle nigga
Goes for all y'all
(let me explain)
It's beauty in the struggle, ugliness in the success
Hear my words or listen to my signal of distress
I grew up in the city and though some times we had less
Compared to some of my niggas down the block man we were blessed
And life can't be no fairytale, no once upon a time
But I be God dammed if a nigga don't be tryin'
So tell me mama please, why you be drinking all the time?
Does all that pain he brought you still

linger in your mind?
Cause pain still lingers on mine
On the road to riches listen this is what
you'll find
The good news is nigga, you came a long
way
The bad news is nigga, you went the wrong
way
Think being broke was better.

J. Cole's *Love Yourz* played as I pulled up to the trap house in Bankhead. Dez called me and Ky and let us know that another one of our workers was missing, and instead of sending his body parts to his family, they had sent it to the Bankhead trap.

"What's good nigga? You ain't have to roll, I know you going through some shit right now," Ky told me as we dapped each other up.

"It's straight man, I had to leave the hospital, I was feeling so damn worthless there."

"He gon' be straight man, just have some faith." I didn't reply as we walked in the house. Dez was sitting at the round table with Brandon, and Rell sitting on the sofa. In front of Dez was a brown box. I walked over to the box and looked inside it.

"Dog, whoever this nigga is, is sick as hell!" I said, stepping back. Inside the box was the lil' nigga tongue, all ten fingers, and one of his eye balls.

"Man, we gotta find out who doing this shit, Dez tell all them niggas to be on guard, and put they ears on the streets, and let them niggas know not to go nowhere alone," Ky said as he walked out the door before Dez could respond.

"Yo, we gotta handle this shit for real," I told him.

"I'm one step ahead of you. But you gotta deal with ya son."

"I know man, but I'm good. I can handle both of them," I told him as I looked across the street and noticed a familiar face. I walked a lil' closer to the street to make sure it was really her.

"Ma?" I called out. The woman looked up from the nigga she was talking to, and looked over at me; when she saw me, she had a shocked look on her face. I never really saw my moms in person, because before my pops was murdered, he used to show me pictures of her all the time. Of course, when I saw pictures of her, she was looking better than she looked now. I walked over to her with Ky following behind me.

"Ty'Shuan, is that you baby boy?" my moms asked with tears in her eyes.

"Yeah, it's me ma." What are you doing out here? Pops told me you died years back," I told her, eyeing the nigga she was standing next to.

My moms looked a hot ass mess, I could tell that she was on that shit heavy.

"Ma, what the hell happened? Why pops tell me you was dead?" I asked my mom as I sat on the hood of my car, and she was leaning on it.

"Your father was upset that I was no longer in love with him, and I found a man that really appreciated me," she told me as she looked at the nigga she was talking to.

"Ma, what you on?"

"Heroin," she told me, putting her head down in shame. When she told me that, my heart broke into a million of pieces. I can't believe my moms was on that shit.

"Come on ma, let me take you to my crib."

"Nigga my bitch ain't going nowhere with you!" the nigga she was standing with said. Ky pulled out his gun before I could pull mine out, and put it up to the nigga dome.

"Now what was that you was saying, my nigga?" I asked him smirking.

"I wasn't saying shit fam," he said, holding up his hand and backing away.

When I got to my crib Taylor was in the kitchen cooking, and she had the house smelling good.

"You must got a female living here with you," my moms said from behind me.

"Yeah, my future wife stays here with me when she don't have school. Bae, come out here for a minute," I yelled out to Taylor.

"Son, where's your bathroom?"

"Down the hall, second door on the right," I told her.

Taylor walked in the living room wearing a crop top, and some leggins; she was looking good as hell and she ain't have no bra on, so I could see her nipple ring.

"Damn ma, you looking good as hell," I told her as I pulled her closer to me and kissed her.

"What's that smell?" she asked,

scrunching up her face.

"My moms."

"I thought you said she was dead?"

"Shit, I thought she was. That's what pops told me when I was about ten. But I was handling business with Ky when I saw her walking across the street from where I was at," I told her as my moms walked back into the living room.

"YOU BITCH!" Taylor yelled as she charged towards my moms.

"Yo Tay, what you doing ma?" I asked her, grabbing her up before she could get to moms.

"This Mea's ho' ass momma," Taylor told me; she was still trying to get free.

"Tay, baby calm down. Are you sure?"

"Yes I'm sure, before the bitch got hooked on drugs I was over her house every day, she and my momma was best friends," Taylor said with tears in her eyes.

"Is that true?" I asked my momma. She didn't say anything, she just nodded her head, "so you telling me you helped some nigga rape your daughter? You let some nigga rape my fucking sister?" I yelled, not even meaning to do so.

"I'm sorry son. If I wouldn't have helped, he was gon' leave me!" she cried.

"Janice, are you fucking serious right now? You let some man do that to your only fucking daughter so he wouldn't leave you? I can't believe this shit. I'm about to go call Ja'Mea and tell her about this shit," Taylor said, snatching her arm from my hands and walked back into the kitchen.

"Sit the fuck down, and do not, I repeat do not leave out that fucking door, or I'ma kill you myself," I told Janice, meaning every word I spoke.

"Yo Tay, hold up bae."

"What the fuck you mean hold up? That bitch is a no good drug ho', that ho' need to go!"

"I know Tay, but are you sure Mea will be able to do what needs to be done?"

"Trust me, she's gon' do it," she said, dialing Ja'Mea's number.

I leaned against the counter, and listened to Taylor tell Ja'Mea everything Janice said, on the other end of the phone I could hear all the hurt in Mea's voice. I was glad Tay didn't tell her that I was her brother;, I would tell her that on my own.

"Thanks for not saying nothing about her not being sister."

"Mhm, go make sure that bitch still in there," she told me, rolling her eyes.

Chapter Nine
Ja'Mea

I was just getting home from work when Taylor called me and told me I needed to come to Shuan's house as quick as I could. When I asked her why, I did not expect for her to say my mother was over there. I quickly sent Kyrie a text letting him know I was home, and that I was about to head over to Shuan's house.

Kyrie: (7:50PM) "Yea I know, I'm on my way over to pick u up, I'll call you when I'm outside." I tossed the phone on the bed, before stripping down so I could get in the shower.

When I got out the shower, I put some lotion on my body, put on some black True Religion Jeans, a black tank top and my Jordan 13 Low Breds. Once I was dressed, I walked over to the mirror and put my damn hair in a ponytail before I heard somebody knock on the door. I looked out my window and saw Kyrie's car sitting outside. I grabbed everything I needed, including my custom made Berretta.

"You ready?" Kyrie asked me as soon as I

opened the door.

"Yeah."

When we got to Shuan's crib, I was nervous as hell. I didn't know what the first thing was that I would do once I saw Janice.

"You aight lil' ma?" Kyrie questioned as he cut the car off. I nodded my head and got out.

When I got inside, I saw Janice sitting on the floor rocking back and forth. Taylor was sitting in a chair giving her the death stare, and Shuan was pacing the floor.

"How did she end up here?" I asked Taylor; she didn't answer me, she just looked at Shuan.

"I brung her over here, I didn't know she was your mama."

"And how do you know her? Why did you bring her over here?"

"Because she's my mother too," he mumbled.

"What?" I asked, looking from Ty'Shuan to Taylor, then down to Janice. Janice just sat on the floor crying.

"Janice don't just sit there be quiet now, open yo fucking mouth before I kick yo ass in it!" Taylor told her standing up.

"18 years ago, I gave birth to a set of twins. Ja'Mea and Ty'Shuan. A few days after we got home from the hospital, I met this man. It was love at first sight. I went home and told y'alls father I didn't want to be with him anymore, and that I had met my husband and he had to leave my house. Your father told me he wasn't leaving without his children. So we made a deal that I keep the girl, and he took the boy. Once he left out the door, we lost all contact with each other and that was it," Janice said in a low voice. I grabbed my Beretta from my purse and walked over to her, pointing the gun to my head.

"Why did you let him do that to me? Why couldn't you just love me like a real mother would love their daughter?" I asked her as I took the gun off safety.

"I'm sorry Mea, if I didn't let him have his way with you, he was gon' leave me, I couldn't let him leav-"

Pow! Pow!

I let off two shots in her dome before I let her finish that sentence. "Sorry about the mess," I told Shuan before walking out the door, and to Kyrie's car.

"You straight?" Kyrie asked me as he got in the car and started it up; I just nodded my head and leaned it against the window.

When we got to Kyrie's house, the first thing I did was go upstairs, grab some clothes I kept over his house, and hopped in the shower. I stayed in the shower for over an hour crying.

When I got out the shower, Kyrie was sitting up in his bed flicking through the channels.

"You sure you straight lil ma?"

"Yes, I'm fine. I just need to get some rest," I told him as I climbed in the bed, pulled the cover over my head, and was out within the next few minutes.

When I got up the next morning Kyrie wasn't in the bed, nor was he in the house when I walked around looking for him. I called his phone several times, and each time it would ring before I got sent to voice mail. I shook my head and put my phone down on the bed as I walked into the bathroom. I handled my daily hygiene before slipping on some clothes. I grabbed the keys to Kyrie's 2015 Ferrari and walked out the door.

As I drove around, all I could think about is the look on Janice face last night when she was telling her story. My mother wasn't shit, but it still hurt me to have to kill her. I wiped the tears as I continued to drive around.

I ended up at Lenox Square Mall. I guess me doing some retail therapy would some what help me get my mind of the shit. The first store I ended up in was Victoria's Secret, and I spent almost $500 in there. I was mad at myself; instead of me saving money, here I was spending it.

As I was walking out the store, I got a text message from Tay asking me where I was, and I texted her back letting her know I was at the mall. I wasn't paying attention to where I was going and walked into somebody. I fell on my ass, with my bags and phone falling next to me.

"Damn bitch, watch where the fuck you walking next time," I heard a female say. I looked up and Kyrie was standing over me with the same bitch whose ass I beat a few weeks ago, and she was holding a lil' baby that looked just like Kyrie.

I took a deep breath before getting up. I was 2.5 seconds away from beating this bitch ass in front of her damn baby, but that wasn't even in me to be fighting in front of some kids. I looked at Kyrie and he had a shocked look on his face; I guess he wasn't expecting me to see him.

"Hi Kyrie, you didn't tell me you had another baby, he's so handsome," I said, picking up my bags and turning around to the exit. When I got in the car and turned the radio on, August Alsina and Nicki Minaj's *No Love* Remix blared through the speakers, I turned it up and sung along with it

August you know, I'm here to save you
Me and them girls, we ain't the same, boo
You know I hate it, when you leave me
'Cause you love it, then you leave it
But you know how bad I need it
You're so fucking conceited
Why you coming over weeded
You can't treat me like you treat them
Yes, I am the crème de la crème
Yes, I am from one to ten, ten
You frontin' in the streets, keep sayin' we

just friends
You can't front like this ain't way realer
I know you hard, I know that you a killer
I know you started off a dope dealer
But let ya guar down, you niggas know you
feel her, feel her
So what you want, baby?
(All I want is you)
(So what you tryin' do?)

When I got to my condo, Kyrie was blowing my phone up. I left that along with the stuff I brought in the car and went into the house. When I got in the house, Tay was sitting on the sofa with one of her school books in her hand.

"I thought you was staying over Ky's house this weekend?"

"Yeah, change of plans." I said. Tay looked up from her book and looked at me.

"What's wrong?" she asked me. I sat down on the sofa next to her, and told her what happened. "You want me to hurt his ass?"

"Nah, don't even worry about it. When he come over here, give him his car keys and let him know I don't want to see him anymore," I said as I got up from the sofa and walked to my room.

A few days went by and Kyrie was still trying to get in touch with me, but I was ignoring all his calls, and because he would pop up at my condo, I was staying at Taylor's house. I knew she wouldn't tell him where I was, so I was good.

I was walking to my car when I saw somebody leaning against my car. At first I thought it was Kyrie until I got closer and realized it was Jermiah. I tried to run back inside my job, but that nigga was quick. He grabbed me by hair and pulled me towards my car.

"You thought I just was gon' let yo ass leave me? Bitch you should know me better than that. Now get the fuck in this car!" he said in my ear, as he pulled me roughly towards the driver's side of my car. I stood outside the car while he got in, contemplating getting in. "Bitch if you try to run again, I promise I'ma shoot ya dumb ass now," he told me, pointing at the window.

I quickly got in, and as soon as I did, he hit me in my jaw with the butt of the gun. That shit hurt like hell, but there was no way in hell I was gon' let him see that.

"We're going home," he told me, and I

knew what he meant.

The whole drive back to Jermiah's house I was trying to think of a way to get away from his crazy ass, but it was hard trying to think with a damn gun pointing at my head. I pulled into the driveway, and he took the keys out the engine before getting out the car. As he was walking around to my side, I reached under the seat and grabbed the .9 I kept under there. Once he opened the door, I sent a bullet in his leg.

"AHHH SHIT, YOU BITCH!" he screamed as he fell on the ground, holding his leg. I hopped out the car, went through his pockets, and grabbed the wad of money he had in there, along with my car keys. I didn't waste any time in starting the car up and pulling off.

All the way back to me and Tay's condo I was shaking., I couldn't lie, I was spooked as hell. I was not expecting Jermiah to come for me, and I damn sure wasn't expecting him to know where I worked. I shook my head, trying to get myself together as I pulled up in front of the condo.

"What the hell is wrong with you? Why are you bleeding? Why is your hair all over your head?" Tay asked me as she stood up, walking over to me.

"Jermiah, he was waiting for me at my job. When I tried to run away he was already on my ass. He grabbed me by my hair, and dragged me back to my car. He had a gum, he hit me in my jaw with it and told me we were going home. When I pulled up to his house, he grabbed the key from the engine, and walked around to get me out. As he was doing that I grabbed my gun from under the seat and shot him in his leg," I said all in one breath.

"I'm calling Ky," was all she said before walking back over to the sofa and grabbing her phone. I didn't even try to stop her as I walked to my room. I stripped out of my clothes as I walked into the bathroom and turned the hot water on. I looked into the mirror and my lip was swollen. I was mad as hell; I was really gon' kill Jermiah's ass when I saw him again.

After I got out the shower, I wrapped a towel around my body and walked in my room. I turned the light on, turned around, and nearly pissed myself.

"Oh my God, you scared the living hell out

of me," I said to Kyrie, grabbing my chest. His ass was standing in the corner of the room looking pissed off.

He didn't say anything as walked over to the window and looked out it, and I went to put some clothes on. Once I was dressed, I sat on the bed and Kyrie walked over and stood in front of it. He grabbed my face and rubbed my swollen lip. His hand felt so damn soft against my skin.

"I'm sorry Mea," he whispered as he continued to stroke my face.

"It's not your fault. I should have knew Jermiah was gon' come after me."

"I'm not talking about the Miah situation, his ass will be handled. Believe that. I'm talking about for not telling you about Siara and my other son Kyan. He's 6 months old."

"Ain't that the same girl I fought when Tay pulled up on Shuan?" He nodded his head, "And she was also over your other baby mama house, when I went with you to get the kids."

"Yeah, she's Shayreese best friend. Siara never told Shay who the father of her child was. And I don't think she's ever seen Kyan either," he told me, shaking his head.

"I'm still upset with you, but I really do appreciate you for coming over here to check on me."

"Come on Mea, that shit was weeks ago, and I said I was fucking sorry."

"Sorry still don't change the fact that you kept it away from me, playing house with her, and probably still fucking her."

"We are not together, I can fuck" but he didn't finish his sentence.

"Yeah, you're right. We aren't together and you can fuck who you want. Now please get out!" I told him as I got up from the bed and walked into the bathroom.

Chapter Ten
Kyrie

I knew I should have told Mea about Kyan, but hell nobody knew about him, not even my momma or sister, and I damn sure shouldn't have said the shit I said to her when I was at her crib but shit, I was mad as fuck that nigga Jermiah went after her after I let his ass walk away with his life.

"I just put Kyan down for a nap, what are you doing here?" Siara asked me as I walked past her and into my son's room. I packed him some clothes and grabbed his diaper bag before picking him. I walked back into the living room and Siara was sitting down on the sofa looking at her phone.

"Don't have my baby around that bitch neither nigga," she told me. I shook my head before walking out the door.

When I got to Ja'Mea's condo, I grabbed Kyan from his car seat and walked right in without even knocking.

"Damn Ky, you don't know how to knock

nigga?" Tay asked as she walked out the kitchen with a bowl of grapes in her hands, "Aw, is this lil' man? He's so handsome," she said, taking Kyan from my hands as I walked to the back.

I walked in Mea's room, again without knocking. She was standing in front of the full length mirror looking at herself, "what are you doing here?" she snapped. I looked up at her eyes and I could see that she was still angry.

"Get dressed, I'll be in the living room, and lil' ma don't make me come back in here to get you," I told her as I walked out the room.

Thirty minutes later, she walked in the living room wearing some True Religion Jeans, a Nike Just Do It Shirt, and some all-white Forces; she looked good as fuck. I grabbed Kyan from Taylor and walked out the door with Mea following behind me.

When I pulled up to my moms crib, my Tre' were playing in the front yard with my 6 year old niece Kayla-Ann, and my 15 year old nephew Khristen. My momma Shonna and sister Kyla were sitting on the porch watching the kids play.

"Who's who is this?" Ja'Mea asked me. I

didn't answer her, I just got out the car, grabbed Kyan from his car seat and went around to open the door for Ja'Mea.

She was a lil hesitant, but she finally got out the car. I grabbed her hand and walked into the gate as my Tre' noticed me.

"Daddy!" Kylan and Kyrie Jr yelled, dropping their toys. Kyria wasn't even worried about me, she ran straight to Ja'Mea.

"Daddy, who's that baby?" Kyria asked when Ja'Mea picked her up.

"This is your brother Kyan," I told them. Kyrie Jr and Kylan both looked at each other, before looking back at me.

"Really?" Kyrie Jr asked,

"Yes really."

"Is he Mea's son?" Kylan asked me.

"No he's not Mea son. He's my son just like you and Kyrie Jr are my sons, and Kyria is my daughter," I told them as I walked over to the porch, with Mea following me.

"Well hello son, I was wondering when you were gon' stop by," my momma said as I kissed her cheek, "Who might this beautiful lady be?" she asked, looking at Mea.

"Ma, Lala this is my baby Ja'Mea, Ja'Mea this is my mother Shonna and my big head big sister Kyla," I said, introducing them then stepping back.

I was happy Ja'Mea and my momma and sister were getting along. Hell all three of them were mad at me for not telling them about Kyan, but I'm sure they would all get over it eventually.

"I like her, she don't take no mess from yo ass," my momma told me as I helped her clean the dishes after dinner.

"Yeah, I like her too ma, I think she might be the one," I smiled.

"Ky, yo rat ass baby momma just popped up!" Kyla told me as she ran back out the house.

"Kyrie, what is this bitch doing holding my fucking son?" Siara yelled, getting out the backseat of Shay's car. Shay's boyfriend was in the driver seat looking out the window.

"Didn't I tell you about having this bum bitch around my fucking children? Kyrie Jr, Kylan and Kyria, go get y'all shit! Y'all coming with me."

"Bitch, my kids ain't going nowhere with yo unfit ass. Khris, take your sister and cousins in the house, don't come out here for nothing, do you understand me?" I asked my nephew, because I knew it was about to be something.

Khris nodded his head before taking Kyan from Mea and walking in the house with the other kids behind him.

"I know both of y'all rat asses better get the fuck away from my OG crib with that shit!" I said as I walked closer to Siara and Shay, who were both looking past me grilling the shit out of Mea.

"I'm not going nowhere until my motherfucking kids are in this car with me," Shay said as she got louder.

"And I want my fucking son, I told yo ass before you left out my house this morning not to have him around that bitch!" Siara said, nodding her head in Mea's direction.

"Look, I'm not gon' be too many more bitches, so I would advise y'all to watch what the fuck y'all saying, and I don't even know why you standing here talking shit, I know yo ass remember the last ass whopping I gave you," Mea said to Siara as she and my sister came and stood on either side of me.

"Bit-" but before Siara could even finish what she was saying, Ja'Mea had her ass on the ground punching her in her face. Shayreese tried to jump in, but my sister grabbed her up so quick and laid her ass down before she could even hit Mea.

"BAE, GET THIS BITCH OFF ME!" Shay screamed.

Pow! Pow!

Hearing the sounds of gun shots, I grabbed my sister off Shay and Ja'Mea off Siara before putting my body in front of theirs. When I heard tires screeching, I got up just in time to see Shay's car speeding away.

"OH MY GOD! NOOO!" I heard my sister scream. I turned around and she was on the porch holding my momma's body in her arms. I ran to the porch and saw my momma was bleeding from her chest.

"Can I please get an ambulance-" I heard Mea say as she told them my mother's address; I was trying to block the sight from the kids, who had ran to the door, upon hearing Kyla's screaming.

"Y'all go sit down, please," I told them as

I opened the screen door and closed the front door.

Three minutes later, an ambulance and several police cars were pulling up. Neighbors were all standing around trying to figure out what happened, and of course the police were asking questions.

"They're taking her to the hospital, I'm gon' ride with them, y'all meet us down there," Kyla told me. I nodded my head and walked to my car with Ja'Mea on my side.

"Give me your keys, you can't drive like that," she said as she went inside my pocket and grabbed my keys. I got in the passenger seat as she went around to the driver's side.

When we got to the hospital, Kyla was sitting on the floor screaming and crying. Just seeing my sister like that, I knew my mother was gon' before I even made it over to where my sister was at. I fell to the ground and cried. Ja'Mea stood behind me and rubbed my back.

Man, I couldn't believe this shit!

"Look, a doctor is over there talking to Kyla. Come on," Ja'Mea told me as she grabbed my hand. I got up and walked over to where the doctor was trying to get Kyla to calm down.

"What's going on Doc?"

"Are you family?"

"Yes, this is my sister."

"I was just asking if she wanted to come see your mother's body,"

"Yes we want to see her," I nodded my head,

"Okay, but y'all can't go into the room and touch her because it's been ruled as a homicide. I'll send a nurse over here to take y'all back," he said before walking away.

Seeing my momma laying there had me fucked up all in the head. Ja'Mea was leaning on me crying, but Kyla was standing next to me staring off into space.

"You know who that nigga is right?" Kyla asked as we walked out the hospital, towards my car.

"No. Who is he?"

"Derrick, one of the niggas that killed Kyson," she told me, calling my pops by his first name.

"Are you sure? I knew he looked familiar, I just could never figure out where I knew him from."

She nodded her head, "Yeah, I promised I would never, and I mean never forget them niggas faces."

Hearing that one of the same niggas that ended my pops life was the same person responsible for killing my momma had me feeling like shit for real. I hit all my niggas up with a code, letting them know to meet me at our meeting spit. I ain't give a fuck if they were in the middle of doing some important shit, nothing was more important than finding that nigga Derrick and putting two in his head, and I let my niggas know if they didn't show up, that was lights out for them.

"I want in on this," Kyla said as I drove towards my momma's house to drop her and Mea off.

"No," I simply said.

"It's either you let me help you find this nigga, or I do it on my own." I thought about it for a few minutes before shaking my head.

"Call Khris and make sure the kids straight," was all I said as I did an illegal U-turn in the middle of the street.

When I got to the house, all the niggas I texted were standing outside talking amongst themselves. I got out my car, walking right past them and into the house without saying shit to them. I went downstairs to the basement. I sat at the head of the table, as all my niggas filed in and sat in they spots. Ty'Shuan took his seat on my left side, and Dez sat on my right side. Ja'Mea and Kayla stood behind me as I looked around the room at all the niggas that were in there.

I knew without a doubt that every nigga would put they life on the line for mine, and I knew once I told them what happened, they were gon' want blood, and that's what I wanted and needed from them.

"As y'all all know I've been looking for my rat ass baby momma Shay for a few weeks now… today she popped up at my OG crib with my other dumb ass baby momma, Siara. To make a long story short, my dumb ass baby momma's started fighting my woman and my big sister in the midst of that. The nigga they were with, Shay's boyfriend, shot and killed my OG," I told them. I looked over at Shuan, and he was crying.

I knew he would take it hard; when he didn't have anywhere to go, my moms took him in, and he stayed with us until we both came up in the game.

–"What you need us to do?" Toby asked me.

"Put a price on they head, let motherfuckers know they ain't no good if they come back dead all of them need to be alive. And while y'all at it, put a price out on Miah's head too. His ass need to be alive too,'" I told them as I got up from the chair and walked up the stairs.

"Bro, you straight?" Shuan asked me as he fired up a blunt and passed it to me.

"Man, right now I don't even know how to feel. This shit too much for me, how yo lil' nigga doing?"

"He straight, they should have his results back sometime tomorrow. I'm just so ready to find out," he told me, I nodded my head as Ja'Mea and Kyla got in my car.

"My nigga, I'ma get up with you later, I gotta drop Kyla off and get my kids and take them home," I told him as we dapped each other up, then I passed him back the blunt.

I stayed at my OG crib with Kyla until her husband Mack came to get her and the kids. Mack was a lawyer; he was my lawyer to be exact, so when I got back to my OG crib, I texted him and let him know what was going on, and told him I was gon' stay with Kyla until he came. I knew she was in no way shape or form in a condition to drive. After they left, I loaded my Tre' and Kyan up in the car and went back to carry a sleeping Ja'Mea to the car before heading home.

When I got back to the crib, Ja'Mea was up and she helped me carry the kids in the house. I made sure they were all in the bed and still sleeping before I headed to my room. Mea wasn't in the room, but I heard water running, so I knew that's where she was at.

When I walked in the bathroom, Mea was running water in the Jacuzzi Whirlpool bathtub.

"Get in," she told me as she turned the water off. I quickly took my clothes off and walked over to the tub.

"Get in it with me," I told her, grabbing her hand before she could away.

"I don't think that's a good idea."

"Come on lil ma, just get in with me," I told her; she looked at me a few minutes before nodding her head. I stepped in the tub as she took her clothes off; once her clothes were off, I helped her into the tub and pulled her to me.

"Thank you for being here for me right now."

"I honestly wouldn't want to be anywhere else right now, Kyrie."

"I have a cabin in Blue Ridge, I want you to take the kids and head up there tomorrow morning, I'm gon' send Toby and Tay up there with y'all."

"I'm not going anywhere Kyrie, I'm gon' be by your side until this is all over with. I'm ridin' for you," she told me, and when she said, that my dick got brick hard. It was on semi hard feeling her body on mine, but her saying that shit did something to me.

I didn't say anything else, I just grabbed her face and kissed her forcefully. She let out a moan as my hands roamed all over her body. I lifted her lil' ass up and sat her on the edge of the tub, and got down low until I was face to face with her pussy. I looked up at her, and she had a look of seduction on her face. I smirked at her, before going in for the kill.

I was nibbling, sucking, kissing, and flicking my tongue on her ass for about three minutes before I felt her legs shaking, then her body started shaking like she was having a seizure.

"Shiiiittttt!" she yelled out as her body fell back down in the tub. I looked down at her ass and smirked.

"Ain't shit funny."

"Come sit on this dick," I told her as I sat down. She smiled before straddled me.

I could feel how tense her body was. "You good lil' ma?" I asked her, and she nodded her head yeah, but the look on her face told me something different.

"Come on, let's go in the room," I told her as she got up, I got out the tub before helping her out. Once she was out, I picked her up and carried her bridal style to my bed.

I gently laid her down on the bed, climbed on top of her and began kissing her deeply. The entire time we were kissing each other, our eyes never left each other. I stared into her eyes and reached down to guide my dick into her love box. When I entered her, I felt her tense up again.

"You want me to stop?"

She nodded her head no. "Just take it slow."

Slowly, I entered her and started to stroke in her.

I picked up the pace and her lil' ass was matching me thrust for thrust.

"Fuck!" I yelled out. It took everything in me not to bust; I had to stop for a few seconds before I started back up again.

"Oh my God! Yes! Right there, don't stop," Mea moaned as she started scratching the hell out of my back. "Damn Ky, I'm 'bout to cum," she told me.

"You is? Then cum for me," I told her as her body started shaking and jerking, again.

"Shit, I'm about to cum with you lil' ma," I told her; there was no way in hell I could have held on any longer.

I released all of my seeds inside of her before rolling over and laying on my back. A few minutes later, she went into the bathroom. I heard the water running; five minutes later, she came out with a wet towel. She wiped my dick off before going back in the bathroom. She came back out and climbed in the bed and snuggled up close to me.

"I love you Ja'Mea," I whispered.

"I love you too, Kyrie."

Chapter Eleven
Taylor

"Your son has a disease called Chronic Granulomatous Disease. It's a genetic disorder in which his immune system cells are not able to kill off certain types of bacteria and fungi. The disease can lead to your son having chronic and long term infections."

"Is there a cure for this?"

"Because we caught the disease early, we can treat it with antibiotics," the doctor told us. I looked over at Ty'Shuan and could see the tears fall from his eyes. I grabbed his hand and let him know that I was there with him every step of the way.

"When will he be able to come home?" Arneisha asked.

"Right now he's getting the treatment as we speak, so if all goes well, he'll be able to go home within the next few days," the doctor told us.

Ty'Shuan thanked him, shook his head, then he walked away. Nene turned her attention to me and Ty'Shuan; I rolled my eyes at the bitch and went and sat down.

"Shuan, I thought I asked you not to bring this bitch back up here," I heard her say before I sat down. I took a deep breath before sitting down. I guess the bitch forgot the last ass whopping I gave her dumb ass.

"Arneisha shut the fuck up bitch! I'm not trying to hear that bullshit. She's gon' be around my kids regardless."

"No the hell she not,"

"Arneisha, I swear on everything I love, bitch if you don't stop talking to me I'ma be going to jail tonight," Ty'Shuan told her, stepping in her face.

"Come on Ty'Shuan, let's go get something to eat." I grabbed his hand, and I was glad he let me walk him out the front door.

I couldn't lie, spending all the time I was with Ty'Shuan was really starting to get to me. Everything we're doing now, from playing the game together, to going to the movies, going out to eat and having picnics in the park, was just like the last time before we made things official between us. I knew he wanted us to get back together, but I still was hurt by the fact another woman had his children.

I wanted to be the first and only female that had his child. But I couldn't be. Somebody else took that away from me, and I swear, I hated that bitch Arneisha with a passion. Before Mea got with Ky, I beat Arneisha's ass on several occasions when she used to play on my phone and let me know that she and Ty'Shuan was fucking around. I never believed her, because I knew she was just another thirsty Thot that wanted what I had, so I never told Ty'Shuan about her calling me, but every time I saw her ass some where, I beat her ass on the spot. Yeah she was the mother of his children, but I was still gon' beat the bitch ass.

Ty'Shuan and I aren't together right now, but that don't mean I won't be there when he needs me. Hell, he was there when I needed him.

"Ty'Shuan, did you ever have feelings for her?" I asked him as we got into my car.

"What? Where the fuck is that coming from, Taylor?"

"I mean, I've just been wondering. I mean you did fuck her raw, right? So that means you must have some type of feelings for the girl, or at least trusted her ass."

"Look Taylor, I don't have feelings for the bitch, I never did. And hell no, I don't trust the hoe. I'm not gon' lie, I hit her raw a few times when I was drunk and you would refuse to come get me. I would call her, and she would come get me."

"How is Ky doing?" I asked him, changing the subject. I was tired of talking about the bitch Arneisha already.

"He good I guess, he just want some payback," he told me, texting away on his phone. I wanted to ask his ass who was he texting in my face, but then when I thought about it, we were not together. He could text who he wanted to.

I couldn't believe it when Ty'Shuan came over to my house and told me about Ky's mama. I met her a few times, and she was a really nice woman. She would always get on Ty'Shuan's head about cheating on me and treating me bad. When he told me that she was dead, I couldn't do anything but cry.

We ended up going over to Ky's house. Ty'Shuan wanted to see how he was holding up, and he also wanted to tell him about Ty'Shuan Jr.

"How is he doing?" I asked Mea as we sat in the TV room.

"I don't know, he say he's fine. But I can tell he's not. I don't think he'll be fine until after he finds them."

"How are you doing? I don't think I asked you that after that shit with Janice."

"I don't have any feelings toward that situation, I mean after it all happened I felt a lil bad, but that quickly faded away when I thought about what she's done." I could tell Mea was hurt by what she did to her mother, but she was never gon' let me know it, even though I was her best friend.

"Where are the kids?"

"They're with Kyla. Well, not Kyria, she refused to leave the house so she's upstairs taking a nap," she laughed.

Ty'Shuan and I stayed over there with Ky and Mea until 12 at night. I was so glad to be home and in my bed; it felt like I hadn't been in my bed in so long well, that is the truth, because I've been spending the night with Ty'Shuan at the hospital. As soon as I laid my head down on the pillow, I was knocked out.

The next day when I woke up, it was nearly three in the afternoon. I rolled over and realized Ty'Shuan ass was sleeping next to me. I most definitely don't remember his ass going to sleep next to me last night. I got out the bed and walked into the bathroom so I could get in the shower, then fix me something to eat. I was hungry as hell.

Once I got out the shower, Ty'Shuan was no longer in the bed. He was now sitting at the countertop, drinking Hennessey straight from the bottle.

"Ty'Shuan, yo ass probably haven't eaten anything, and the first thing yo ass wanna do is drink?" I snatched the bottle from his hand and put it down on the counter.

"I'm stressed ma, this shit is just too much for a nigga."

"I know Ty'Shuan, but drinking isn't gon' solve any of your problems and you know that," I told him as he pulled me closer to him.

"I need you ma, I can't lose you."

"Ty'Shuan, I'm still here baby. But I just can't be with you right now,-" I told him, backing out of his embrace.

"Come on, why not?"

"Because you cheated on me, and got the girl pregnant, then you lied to me about you fucking with the bitch." I was really trying to keep my calm, but his ass was really pushing it right now.

He didn't reply, he just picked the bottle back up and took a swing, I didn't tell his ass nothing this time there was nothing I could tell him. He was still gon' do what the hell he wanted to do. I just went into the kitchen to fix me something to eat.

****

Three days later, it was the day of Ky's mama's funeral. I swear, this was not something I was ready for. I rode in the family car with Ky, Ja'Mea, Kyla, Kyla's husband Mack, Ty'Shuan and the kids. It was a quiet car ride except for the sniffles from everyone in the car.

After the service, we were all standing at her grave site. I was standing next to Ty'Shuan holding his hand, Ja'Mea was holding Ky's hand, and Mack was holding Kyla up. I felt bad for her, but I knew her pain all too well. Just four years ago, I lost my mother, and although she didn't get murdered, she died of cancer and the pain was still there.

We were walking back to the family car when an all-black van pulled up in front of us. Before I could say anything, shots rang out and I was thrown to the ground. All I heard was screaming as I saw people either fall to the ground, or get pushed down. I looked around for Ja'Mea and saw that Ky was on top of her body.

As quick as the shots started, they stopped. Ty'Shuan waited a few extra minutes to get off me and help me up from the ground.

"You alright?" he asked me as I dusted myself of. I nodded my head and looked at Mea; Ky was helping her up off the ground.

"Mack check on the kids," Ky told him as him and Mea walked over to where we were standing.

"Yo, y'all straight?" Ky asked us.

"Yeah we're good, man you good though?"

"You know I' am. But I'ma be even better when I find out the niggas who did that shit," he said, pulling out his phone and walking towards the family car.

We all ended up at one of Ky's houses in Bankhead. He was pissed as hell somebody shot up his mama's funeral, but who couldn't blame him. Whoever did it didn't give a fuck about nobody. There were kids and innocent people out there.

"I DON'T GIVE A FUCK MAN! IF YOU DON'T FIND OUT WHO DID THAT SHIT YOU MIGHT AS WELL GET YO MAMA THAT BLACK DRESS BECAUSE I'MA KILL YA DUMB ASS!" Kyrie screamed into the phone. Mea walked over to him, whispered in his ear, and of course his ass calmed down. He sat down on the sofa and put his head in his hand.

I loved the fact that all it took was for Mea to tell him something, and he would instantly calm down. Just by the way Mea would look at Ky, I knew she was in love already and I was happy for my best friend. I was just glad she was finally over Jermiah's lying no good ass.

Finally, after Ty'Shuan and Ky handled business and talked to their niggas, Ty'Shuan and I were finally heading home. I couldn't wait to get in the shower and get in my bed, well Ty'Shuan's bed because there was no way in hell he would let me go home to my house. He was gon' be sleeping in one of his guest rooms, because I knew if he slept in the bed with me he was gon' try to have sex with me, and I couldn't take it there with him. We were just friends, nothing more and nothing less.

"Can I get a massage when we get home?" he asked me as we stopped at a stop light; I looked up from my phone and looked at him.

"No nigga, but you are sleeping in your guest room," I told him; he chuckled like some shit was funny, but I didn't find shit funny with what I said. I was dead ass serious.

Just as he was about to say something, a black van pulled up on his side. It was the same van from earlier and before I could warn him, shots ran out. Ty'Shuan pressed down on the gas as the person was still shooting at us.

We turned down a side street, and the shooting finally stopped.

"Yo you good ma?" he asked me.

"Yes, but you're bleeding," I told him; he looked down at his shirt and shrugged his shoulders.

"I'm straight ma," he said, pulling off.

Chapter Twelve
Shayreese

I don't know what the fuck I was thinking getting involved with a nigga like Derrick. His ass wasn't shit but the devil. I should have left his ass when he started beating Kyrie Jr and Kylan, but I was dumb in love with his ass; now I'm stuck with his crazy ass.

I hated Kyrie's ass with a passion, but there was no way in hell I wanted to see him dead, because the fact still remained that no matter how much I hated his ass, I still loved him and he was still a wonderful father to Kyrie Jr, Kylan, and Kyria, and now he was a wonderful father to Siara's son Kyan.

I knew Kyrie thought I didn't know anything about the lil relationship him and Siara had behind my back, but I knew everything. Siara came clean to me about it way before she knew she was pregnant. I was cool with it; although I loved Ky's ass more than anything in this world, I knew we would never be together anymore and the only reason he was still dealing with me was because of the kids

"Bitch, I know yo dumb ass hear me talking to you!" Jermiah's ugly ass said as he smacked me upside my head.

"Jermiah, you put yo fucking hands on me one more time, I promise I'ma do what that dumb bitch of yours failed to do!" I rolled my eyes at Jermiah; he was starting to be a pain my ass.

"Did y'all handle that?"

"Yes Jermiah! Damn. Derrick is getting rid of the van right now," I told him as I walked downstairs to the basement. I had to get away from his ass before I really did kill him.

When Jermiah found out Derrick had some type of beef with Kyrie, he reached out to me and had me get him in contact. Of course, Derrick told Jermiah all about his plan to take Kyrie and Shuan out to take over there business. Derrick wanted to take over when he killed Kyrie's father years ago, but he couldn't because Kyrie stepped up to the plate.

Yes, when I first got with Derrick I knew what his intentions were; I knew he wanted to kill Kyrie, and at the time I didn't give a damn, but that shit he pulled to-day at Ms. Shonna's funeral had me tripping hard. I can't believe he shot at that damn funeral, especially with all those innocent people out there. I was so lucky my babies weren't out there, because if something would have happened to them, I was gon' fasho kill Derrick's ass.

"Yo baby, you down here?" I heard Derrick yell down the stairs.

"Yeah."

"What you doing down here?" he asked as he walked over to the sofa where I was sitting.

"I had to get away from Jermiah, he been getting on my nerves. I wish his leg hurry and heal so he could go out and do this shit himself. I mean, you know I'm always down to ride with you, but I'd rather not be behind killing innocent people!" I said and before I knew it, Derrick had my ass pinned against the wall choking the hell out of me.

"You thinking about leaving me bitch?" he asked me as spit flew from his mouth; I shook my head no. "That's what the fuck I thought," he told me as he let me go and let my body dropped to the ground.

Chapter Thirteen
Jermiah

I didn't give a fuck what I have to do, but I was gon' get Ja'Mea's ass back one way or another. I know I had a fucked up way of showing it, but I loved her; she was the love of my life. My childhood was so fucked up that I didn't really know how to show my love. I didn't know what the hell was wrong with me, but anytime I had a problem that I couldn't handle on the street, I took my frustrations out on her ass.

The first time I ever beat her ass is when I stole some money and work from Ky and Shuan. I don't know how they knew, but a few days later they figured out it was me, and they beat my ass. Then after they beat my ass they had some of they lil' niggas do the same thing. When I went home that night, Mea was so worried about me, but after I told her what happened, I felt embarrassed as hell, so I beat her ass.

Seeing Ja'Mea walk around the city with that nigga Ky had me feeling some type of way, and I was gon' get my bitch back if it was the last thing I did. I was gon' slowly watch Ky's empire fall to the ground with the help of Derrick, then I was gon' take his ass out, then swoop in and get Mea back.

Whenever I saw her out, I could never get close to her because Ky always had somebody following behind her, even if it was at work or school. Somebody was always there with her. I was still pissed at her as for shooting me in my leg, and when I did get my hands on her, she gon' pay for doing that dumb ass shit.

"Yo you ready to do this? Shayreese tied up downstairs," Derrick asked me as he walked in the kitchen where I was fixing me something to eat.

"Yeah, let me finish up this sandwich. I'm hungry as hell," I told him.

"Nigga hurry the fuck up, we don't have time for this shit, we need to hurry up before one of them niggas get back to the house."

We were going to hit up another one of their trap houses, and this time we were taking everything, and not just the money we wanted everything in the house, and that included work and them niggas lives.

Chapter Fourteen
Kyrie

When I got that call from Shuan, telling me that somebody shot his car up, I was 38 hot. I was so glad I had Ja'Mea here by my side, on some real shit. She was the very thing I needed to calm me down, and all it took was for her to tell me three words, but right now I was so damn irritated that I couldn't even be around her.

"Where are the kids?" Ja'Mea asked me as she walked into the bathroom, as I was stepping out the shower.

"Mack's sister Maye came got them early this morning. She's taking them up to Ridgewood."

"And why didn't you take wake me up so I could say bye?" she snapped, putting her hands on her hip. I knew it was about to be some shit in here.

"Come on Mea, don't start that shit right now," I told her, walking out the bathroom and into the room.

Her ass was right on my heels as I walked

162

in the closet to find me something to wear. Ever since I started putting the dick game down on the regular, her mouth had become too damn reckless for me. I mean, she already didn't have a filter before the dick. The shit just got worse when I started laying the pipe down on her ass, though.

"Start what shit Kyrie? All I asked was why you didn't wake me up before the kids left."

"Because you were sleeping so peaceful Mea, I didn't want to disturb you."

"That's bullshit and you know it," she said as she walked out the closet.

She wasn't lying; the shit I just told her was some straight up bullshit. I didn't wake her up because I didn't want her to meet Maye. I used to fuck with Maye heavy before I met Ja'Mea, but I stopped fucking with her when I realized I wanted and needed Ja'Mea in my life. Don't get me wrong, Maye would still suck me up from time to time, but that was about it. She couldn't get nothing else from me.

When I told her I couldn't fuck with her anymore, she threw that she was pregnant card out on the table. She showed me some papers and her ass was indeed pregnant, but that didn't mean the baby was mine, so until the baby came, I ain't want shit to do with her ass.

I know if I would have let Ja'Mea and Maye meet earlier, it was bound to be some shit, and that's something I didn't need on my plate right now. I was already pissed that Kyla had Maye come get the kids, instead of her getting them herself.

When I got dressed, I walked downstairs and Ja'Mea was putting her hair in a ponytail. She looked so fucking good wearing some Robin jeans, a half shirt that showed off her toned stomach, and a fresh pair of all white Forces.

"Where you think you're going?" I asked her as I watched her pick her keys up from the table.

"I do have a damn job, and I am in school," she told me as she rolled her eyes at me.

"Ja'Mea, don't walk yo ass out that fucking door," I told her calmly, and of course, she ignored my ass and walked out the door anyway. I took my phone out as I walked over to the bar. I poured me a shot of vodka, then texted Dez.

Me: (2:15PM) "Yo Dez let Toby take the car so he can follow Ja'Mea for me. You can ride with me,"

Dez B.: (2:16PM) Fasho"

Thirty minutes later Dez, and I were walking in Onyx. I had so much shit on mind and I just needed to get it off.

"Hey Dez, hey Ky. Can I get y'all something?" Scandalous asked as –she walked over to us.

"What up Scan? Nah, I'm straight ma."

"What about you Ky? Can I get you something?" she asked me, licking her lips.

"It's not something you can get me, it's more of something you can do for me," I told her smirking, she grabbed my hand and led me to the back of the club.

Thirty minutes later, I was walking from the back, zipping up my pants.

"Yo you one dirty nigga," Dez laughed as I sat next to him.

"I don't give a fuck what y'all niggas say, but that bitch got some good ass head," I laughed. Everybody knew Scandalous' reputation for setting niggas up, but her ass never tried that shit with me. In fact, she actually helped my lil' niggas out when they wanted to set up some niggas.

"Uh, Ky," Dez said, looking up from his phone, and at me with a worried expression on his face.

"What?"

"T just hit me up and said yo girl is at Roscoe's with some nigga, and the-" that was all I allowed that nigga to say before I hopped up and was out the door.

When I pulled up to Roscoe's, I sat in my car, across the street from the place, watching as Ja'Mea was entertaining some nigga. I wasn't gon' go in there and act a fool, that was until I saw him reach across the table and stroke the side of her face.

I got out the car and walked in there with Dez following behind me, Toby got out his car just as I walked past the car. I walked into the place and all eyes were on me. I was glad Ja'Mea's back was toward me; I didn't want her to see me coming.

"I don't really know anything more about it," Ja'Mea said as I stood behind her, the nigga she was talking to looked up at as if he had a fucking problem. Slowly Ja'Mea turned around and looked up at me, and the look on her face was fucking priceless. If I wasn't so mad at her ass, I would have laughed at the way she was looking right now.

"Ky-Ky, this is-" she was stuttering, trying to get the words out, but I stopped her ass.

"Save it, get yo ass up and get home now. And I swear Ja'Mea if you don't make it there before I do, you gon' have a problem!" I told her, never taking my eyes off the nigga she was sitting with.

"Nigga I don't know who the fuck you think you talking to, but we're having a conversation."

"Conversation ended nigga!" I told him, pulling my 9 out, and sitting on the table. "Ja'Mea, I promise I'm not gon' tell yo ass again. Get the fuck up and get yo ass home," I told, her raising my voice. This time, she got u and walked out the door, "Nigga I'm gon' tell you this one time, and one time only, get the fuck outta town, because I promise, if I ever see you again, I'ma end ya life," I told him, turning around and walking out.

When I got home, Ja'Mea was upstairs in my room, packing her clothes.

"Where the fuck you think you're going?" I asked as I grabbed the clothes from her hand and threw them back on the bed.

"Kyrie, please leave me the fuck alone," she said with tears in her eyes.

"Ja'Mea, I'm not letting you leave me lil' ma. I can't do it,." I told her as I grabbed the clothes out the bag she was packing and tossed them back on the bed.

"Go fuck whatever bitch you was fucking with earlier," she said as she looked up at me.

"What the hell are you talking about?"

"So you gon' stand here and play dumb with me?" she asked, walking up to me. I couldn't lie, the look on her face had me spooked as hell.

"I really don't kno-" but before I could finish my sentence, her ass was punching me in my face. I couldn't lie, her punches were hurting. I grabbed her hand and pinned her ass against the wall.

"Ja'Mea, don't fucking put yo hands on

me again man," I told her through clenched teeth.

"Fuck you!" she said as she kneed me in the balls. I doubled over and her ass tried to walk away, but before she could get far, I grabbed her by her hair, pinned her against the wall and had her choked up.

"Ja'Mea, calm down lil' ma."

"Let me the fuck go!" I let one of her hands go, and she slapped the shit out of me. I punched the wall above her head; she really had me fucked up if she think I was some bitch ass nigga that was gon' let her hit me constantly.

"So what, you gon' hit me? Go ahead do it. Show me you're no different than Jermiah," she said as the tears rapidly fell from her eyes. I let her go and she fell to the ground. Hearing the shit that just came out her mouth fucked my head up. I looked at her for a few minutes, before walking out the room and downstairs to the bar; I needed a drink.

Ja'Mea really fucked my head up if she thought I was anything like that fuck nigga Miah. I sat at the bar, throwing shot after shot back. I knew before long I was gon' be drunk as hell. I heard her coming down the stairs as I poured another shot. I felt her standing right behind me, so I turned around. She had tears streaming down her face.

"Kyri-" she started, but I held up my hand. I didn't want to hear shit she had to say right now. I took another shot and got up from the bar, walking upstairs. I know I was being childish for the shit I was doing right now, I know I should have been talking to her, but fucked that I pissed off, and she was gon' know it.

Chapter Fifteen
Ja'Mea

I know I shouldn't have said the bullshit I said to Kyrie about him being anything like Jermiah, but I was mad as hell. I guess he thought he was just gon' cheat on me with some stripper bitch and I wasn't gon' find out, but of course the ho' couldn't keep it to her-self. She couldn't wait to let it be known that she fucked with Kyrie. I'm guessing right after Kyrie left, her thirsty ass she uploaded the video of her sucking his dick to Facebook and Instagram and it just so happened I was her friend on Facebook and following her ass on Instagram.

I don't even know what made me look at the video when she posted it, but when I did, I got the shock of my life when I saw the birthmark in the shape of a heart on Kyrie's dick, then what really let me know it was him was hearing his voice when he told her to *'suck that shit just like that'* and him saying he was about to cum. I don't even think he knew she was recording him, but that's not the point. His ass shouldn't have been fucking with the bitch in the first place.

The shit I said to him, yeah I know it shouldn't have came out of my mouth. There is no doubt in my mind, I know Kyrie is nothing, and I mean nothing at all like Jermiah. I said the shit I said out of anger and frustration, and his ass should have known that, but of course, his ass wanted to be stubborn and ignore me like a lil' fucking kid. He wouldn't answer none of my calls, and his ass wouldn't even text me back. After a week of getting no reply from him, I just said fuck it and gave up. I was no longer about to kiss his ass, when I had more important shit to worry about.

"What the hell is wrong with you? You sitting here looking like yo lost yo best friend," Tay said –to me as she walked into our condo with some bags in her hand. I was sitting on the sofa eating grapes and trying to study for my last final of the semester, but I was having no such luck; all I could think about was Kyrie.

"Nothing."

"Girl don't sit here and tell me nothing, I know your ass better than you know yourself.

You miss Kyrie don't you?" she asked me, sitting down on the sofa next to me and grabbing some grapes from my bowl.

"I do miss him, but I refuse to kiss his ass. I know what I said was fucked up and all, but he seem to forget what the fuck he did."

"Mea, are you sure it was him that she was sucking off? I mean, it could have been any nigga."

"The birthmark I saw, yeah it could have belonged to any nigga, it could have been a burn or something, but I know Kyrie's voice. When I heard him say what he said to her, I knew that was him without a doubt," I told her, putting my book down on the table.

"I think both of y'all should just talk. He was wrong for the shit he did, and you were wrong for what you said. You know Ky is not like Jermiah in no way, shape, or form. I love you Ja'Mea, and you know I will never, ever tell you anything wrong," she told me as she got up and walked in the kitchen. I knew she was right, but I wasn't gon' keep reaching out to him only to be ignored.

A few days had went by since the shit with

Kyrie and I, and I couldn't lie, I was missing his ass like crazy, but as I said before, I refused to kiss his ass. One thing I was glad about was my semester finally being over with. Shit, being a full-time student along with being a full-time worker was stressful as hell. It was all starting to become a lil' bit too much for my body to handle. I was starting to feel weaker and weaker as the days went on, but I was still pushing.

I was just getting off work, and walking towards my car when I saw two familiar faces walking in front of me. Neither one of them were paying attention to their surroundings, because they hadn't noticed me following them to the car they were walking to. I looked inside my purse to make sure I had my .9 or my Beretta; I saw my .9 in there, so I watched them get in a car. I ran to my car just as they were pulling out the parking lot. I started my car up, and followed them.

I followed them all the way to Dawson, and I couldn't believe my eyes when I saw Siara pulled up in front of my old house. I watched as she and Seth both got out the car and went into the house. I waited fifteen minutes to make sure neither one of them would come back out the house., When I saw they didn't, I pulled my .9 out and made sure nobody was outside or looking out their windows before walking into the house.

As soon as I stepped a feet through the cracked front door, I felt the need to throw up, but thank God I didn't though. Just being in this house had me thinking about the last time I was here, had me ready to break down and cry, but I kept it together. I closed my eyes before walking towards the kitchen, where I heard the moaning coming from. I peeped my head around the corner, and saw Siara shooting up, and Seth eating her pussy.

I chuckled before taking my gun off safety, and walking into view.

"Yo, what the fuck are you doing here, bitch?" Seth asked me. I guess Siara was so high that she hadn't even noticed I had a gun and was pointing it at her, but Seth did. He stopped eating her pussy and looked up at me like he saw a ghost.

"Why do you look so surprised to see me?" I told him, leaning against the wall, with the gun still pointed at them.

"Wha-wha-what are you doing here? What

do you want?" he asked.

"Shut the fuck up, you bitch made nigga," I told him, sending a bullet in Siara's arm before I killed either one of them. I was gon' make sure they suffered, and I mean suffered real good.

"Bitch are you out of your mind?" Seth asked as he hopped up from the ground, and tackled me to the ground.

The gun fell from my hand, and Seth was trying to get to it, but I kicked his ass in the stomach and picked it up before he did. I was getting back to my feet when Seth punched me in my stomach;, that shit hurt, but I was not about to let that get to me. I shot Seth in his arm, then his leg before he fell down. I shot Siara in her face, then her dome before looking back at Seth. He had tears in his eyes and was looking at me.

"Don't cry now you, bitch ass nigga! Your ass wasn't crying when you were raping, me were? You weren't crying when you were beating me, were you?" I asked, shooting him in his other arm, then his other leg. His ass didn't say anything, he didn't even scream out in pain. I guess his ass was that high that it didn't even hurt him. I looked down at him and smirked before shooting him in his dome, ending his miserable ass life.

My stomach was killing me as I slowly walked back to my car., I don't know why I was walking so damn slow when I heard the police sirens coming towards my direction. Once I was finally in my car, I took a sigh of relief; before pulling off and heading home.

When I got home, I silently thank God Taylor wasn't there. I really did not feel like telling her what I did, although I know she wouldn't be mad at me, but she would be upset that I followed them by my damn self. I also didn't feel like telling her that one of Kyrie baby mama's were doing drug and fucking Seth. I walked into my bathroom and turned the shower on.

Being back in that house brought up so many memories, and I felt so disgusted and nasty just being back in there. I stood in the shower, feeling sick as hell. I felt myself about to throw up, and this time; I knew it was going to come up. I got out the shower and threw up all over the floor. Weakly, I got up and cleaned the floor; before getting in the shower again.

When I got out the shower I wrapped the towel around my body before walking into my room. When I got in there, Kyrie was sitting on my bed looking at me, and boy, if looks could kill, I would have dropped dead right then and there.

"What the hell is wrong with you, Mea?" he asked, standing up and walking over to stand in my face. He was so close to me, that the smell of his Gucci cologne filled my nostrils.

"What are you talking about Kyrie? And can you back the hell up out my face?"

"You know what the fuck I'm talking about Ja'Mea, you just out here wilding? Doing shit on your own now? What if something would have happened to you while you were out there killing people?"

"Look, don't worry about me Kyrie, what you need to be worried about is why your baby mama was out there doing drugs with Seth's nasty ass," I spat as I pushed him and walked over to the dresser to get me something to put on.

"I don't give two fucks about her ho' ass and you know that Ja'Mea, I'm more worried about why yo ass out here doing wild shit like that? Especially with that nigga Miah still out there and looking for you, what if he would have saw you and grabbed yo ass up man? What the fuck was you gon' do?"

"Oh, so wait, now you give a fuck?" I snapped.

"Don't do that bullshit Ja'Mea, you know I care about what happens to yo ass. If I didn't give a fuck I would have just kept walking when the nigga Miah had you choked up outside that damn club," he told me as he grabbed my arm, turning me around and pinning me against the wall next to the dresser.

"So tell me, did you give a fuck about me when you were fucking that stripper bitch? Huh? Did you Kyrie?" I asked as the tears welled up in my eyes and rapidly fell.

Of course his ass didn't answer me, he just let my arms go and walked out the room.

"That's what the fuck I thought!" I yelled as he slammed my room door. I put on me some clothes, then got in my bed. I knew he wanted me to follow him, but there was no way in hell I was gon' do that; as soon as my head touched the pillow I was out like a light.

The next morning when I woke up, Kyrie was lying next to me as if everything was all good between us; I sat up and just looked at him. He was so handsome, and just looking at him sleep had me wanting to pull his basketball shorts down, hop on his dick, and ride it.

I got wet just thinking about him being inside of me.

"Why are you staring at me?" Kyrie asked me without even opening his eyes.

"I wasn't staring at you," I lied.

"You don't gotta lie," he told me as he turned over on his side and looked at me.

"Why are you here? Don't you have a bed of your own?"

"Yeah, I do have a bed of my own, but you're not in it, so I'm here where you at."

"Well I wish you would have went to your bed," I told him as I laid back down and turned my back on him.

Kyrie pulled me closer to him, and kissed the back of my neck.

"You really wish I was at home in my own bed? Or laying right here with you?" he asked as he stuck his hand in my leggings and started playing with my clit. Even though I didn't mean to, I moved my leg over to give him more access, "do you really want me to stop?" he asked as he stuck two fingers in me. I didn't say anything as he started sucking and biting on my neck.

Just as I felt myself about to cum, his cell phone rung. He kissed my neck once more before removing his fingers and reaching for his phone. I wanted to punch his ass in the face. I got out the bed and walked into the bathroom just as he answered the phone. I turned the shower on, then got in.

When I got out the shower, I walked into my room with the towel wrapped around my body; Kyrie had fell back to sleep. I put some clothes on, then went into the living room where Shuan and Tay were sitting playing the Xbox One.

"Where my boy at?" Shuan asked me as I sat down on the sofa with Tay.

"In my bed sleeping, why don't you go get him and take him some where?"

"Nah we chilling right now.,"

"Why can't y'all chill some where else, I don't want his ass here."

"So you don't want me here, huh?" Kyrie asked, walking into the living room with his phone in his hand.

"Nope."

"Well yo ass wasn't just saying that whe-" he was saying, but I gave him the look of death.

"Ah shit, y'all was up there being nasty?" Tay asked as they all laughed, but I didn't find shit funny.

Chapter Sixteen
Kyrie

I don't even know why Ja'Mea ass acting like she still made at a nigga and shit, when she know damn well she's over it and just want me to kiss her ass. Last night when I climbed in the bed with her, her ass cuddled up right next to me.

I know letting that bitch Scandalous suck me up was gon' come back to bite me in the ass, but I ain't give a fuck about that. I just needed to release some stress, and I couldn't do it with Ja'Mea because I refuse to be rough with her. I was still mad at her for having that nigga all up in her face, and I was pissed off for her doing that dumb shit she did with that bitch Siara and Seth.

I knew all about that bitch doing drugs and fucking with some nigga named Seth, but I never knew the nigga was the same nigga that raped lil' ma. If I did know that, I was gon' end his ass myself, but I was kind of glad Mea got the chance to do it herself I know she needed that.

"Come on lil' ma, when you gon' stop

acting like this with me?" I asked her as I sat down on her bed, pulling her between my legs as she was walking to her bathroom.

"Why did you let her suck your dick? Is it because I don't do it how you like it?" she asked, putting her head down.

I lifted her up, and she put it right back down.

"Look at me lil ma," I told her; it took her a few minutes, but she finally put her head up and looked at me. "You're the best I ever had, when it comes to sex, when it comes to love, period. I haven't had anybody like you and I don't want anybody like you. In the short time that I've known you I've fallen in love with you, and I don't regret anything. I'm sorry for even letting that bitch suck me off, my intentions were never to hurt you, and I'm sorry you even found out about it," I told her as I kissed her lips.

"I'm sorry about what I said too, I know you're in no way, shape, or form anything like Jermiah, I should have never said that."

"It's cool ma, I know you were upset, but you did fuck my head up with that shit," I told her as she sat down on my lap.

"Speaking of Jermiah, what are we gon' do about it?"

"I'm gon' handle him, I don't want you to worry about him anymore, I just want you to sit back and chill."

"I can't do that."

"What you mean you can't do that?"

"I can't Kyrie, Jermiah put me through so much shit while we were together. I just can't sit back. I want to kill his ass myself."

I didn't reply to her; I wasn't sure how I felt about her committing another murder. I mean, when she already killed her mother, without even blinking, then she killed two more people, I was starting to think her mama wasn't the first body she caught.

"What you thinking about?" she asked me with a worried expression on her face.

"Can I ask you something?" I asked her; she nodded her head while looking me in my eyes.

"Was your mama the first person you ever killed?" I asked her; she looked at me for a few more minutes before finally looking down at the floor, shaking her head no. "Who was it?"

"Me and Shuan's father. I saw him out one day at a grocery store. I walked up to him, and I explained to him what was going on with me, and how my mama was treating me. He told me he didn't give a fuck and he couldn't do anything for me unless I let him fuck me," she cried into my chest. I rubbed her back as she cried.

That's one thing I loved about Ja'Mea; she's been through a lot in her life, but you wouldn't know it unless you knew her. She didn't walk around bitter like most people who'd been through what she had. She walked around with a smile on her face no matter what the situation was.

"Shh, it's gon' be straight lil' ma. You did the right thing, that fuck nigga didn't deserve to live," I told her, I never liked his ass anyway, he always had some smart shit to say about both me and Shuan, and Shuan was his flesh in blood.

"I killed him, and Shuan is gon' hate me," she cried even harder.

"Lil ma', Shaun is not gon' hate you. Go wipe your face and get your self together, and meet me downstairs," I told her as she slightly pushed off me.

When I got downstairs, Shuan and Tay were still playing the game. I swear I don't even know why he cheated on her with that rat bitch Nene, or Shanice.

"You know man, if y'all just don't go ahead and get married something wrong with y'all niggas," I told them as I sat down on the sofa.

"No, we're okay just being friends right now," Tay told me.

I looked over at Shuan and I knew his ass didn't feel the same way. I was gon' give they asses a few more weeks before they got back together. I don't even know why Tay was playing like she wasn't still in love with him.

"Y'all, pause the game, I gotta tell y'all something, well Tay you probably already know about it," I told them; both of them paused the game and looked at me. I told them everything Mea told me.

As I finished telling them, Mea walked down the stairs; she was still crying and her face was still puffy. Shuan got up from the floor where he was sitting, and walked over to her and hugged her.

"I'm not mad at you sis, that nigga wasn't a good pops, so don't feel bad. You actually did me a favor," Shuan told her as he let her go, then kissed her on the cheek. She walked over to me and looked me in my eyes.

"Thank you."

"You don't have to thank me lil' ma," I said, leaning down to kiss her lips.

"Aye, take that shit some where else. Don't nobody want to see that shit,." Tay laughed as my phone rung. I took it out my pocket and saw that it was Maye calling. That bitch had been calling me non stop since last night; I had to turn my damn phone off last night because her ass was blowing it up like something was wrong with her ass.

"I'll be right back lil' ma," I told Ja'Mea before walking out the front door.

"What the fuck you want, Maye?" I asked as I walked down a flight of stairs.

"I want to know what are you gon' do about your child?"

"Kyrie Jr. Kylan, Kyria and Kyan are straight. Them the only kids I got."

"No, you have another one on the way

with me."

"Maye, if you don't get the fuck off my phone with that bullshit, I never fucked yo ass raw. If I even thought I did, then yeah it could have been a possibility that yo baby is mine. But since I know for sure I didn't fuck you raw, and I know I flushed the condom down the toilet, stop playing calling me and go find yo real baby daddy," I told her as I hung up the phone.

When I turned around to walk back up the stairs, Ja'Mea was standing there with tears in her eyes. I couldn't do shit but put my head down as she turned around and walked back up the stairs.

"Shit man," I said as I walked up the stairs.

"Where lil' ma at?" I asked Shuan and Tay, who were now back playing the game.

"She went into her room, slamming the door," Tay said, not even looking up from the TV. I walked to the back and Ja'Mea had locked the door. I shook my head, because I knew either I was just gon' walk away and let her ass be mad, because ain't nobody tell her to follow me, or I was gon' have to kick the damn door down.

"Ja'Mea, can you please open the door?"

"No, just please leave me alone!" she yelled back. I knew I was gon' end up kicking the door down. I refused to have her walking around mad at me again.

"Lil' ma, it's either you open the door, or I kick it down. Now the choice is yours," I told her. I waited five minutes to see if she was gon' get up and open the door. When it's clear that she wasn't, I kicked it down.

"What the fuck did you do that shit for?" she asked, hopping off the bed.

"I gave you two choices, and you chose that one."

"I don't have shit to say to yo ass."

"That's fine, all you have to do is listen to me," I said, grabbing her hand, and walking over to the bed. I sat down and pulled her between my legs as she turned her head to look at the wall. I swear she was stubborn as hell.

"Look, Maye is Mack sister, I fucked with her ass here and there, it was never nothing serious. When I met you, I let her know I couldn't fuck with her anymore, because I found the woman I wanted to spend the rest of my life with. That's when she came at me talking that she pregnant bullshit. She took the test in front of me and everything. But I let her know that there was no way that baby could be for me, because I wore a condom every time I fucked with her."

"Just how many kids do you have, Kyrie?"

"I only have four children. Kyrie Jr, Kylan, Kyria, and Kyan. I promise you Maye's child is not mine," I said as I grabbed her face and pulled it closer to me so I could kiss her. I was glad when she let me kiss her.

"Is that the real reason you didn't wake me up when she came to get the kids? Because you didn't want her to tell me she's pregnant with your kid?"

"That's not my kid, and yeah that's why. I just didn't feel like dealing with all that bullshit." She nodded her head before yanking her arm away from me and getting into her bed.

A week went by and Ja'Mea was still giving me the cold shoulder. We slept in the same bed, but her ass was ignoring me so good. She wouldn't even let me cuddle up with her. That shit was really getting on my last nerves.

It was the middle of the night when I woke up, because somebody phone was vibrating, I didn't know if it was mine or Ja'Mea's, but whoever it was, I chose to ignore it. I laid my head back down and tried to go back to sleep, but whoever was calling just kept calling. I reached over Ja'Mea and picked up my phone. When I realized it wasn't mine, I picked Ja'Mea's up, and somebody name *Low* was calling. His ass was calling back to back at 3 in the morning, so I decided to answer it and see what the fuck he wanted.

"Yo."

"Where is Ja'Mea?"

"She sleeping play boy, what can I do for you?"

"I want to talk to her."

"Nigga didn't I just say she was sleep, nigga?" I said as lil' too loud, because Ja'Mea opened her eyes and looked at me.

"I don't give a fuck if she sleep, wake her ass up!"

"Nigga, you must not know who the fuck this is. Don't call my woman phone no more, because if you do, I promise you regret it," I said, hanging up in his face as Ja'Mea sat up.

"Who was that?" she asked

"Who the fuck is Low?" I asked her; she turned her ahead and looked over toward the window. "Ja'Mea, don't fucking play with me, who is he?"

"He's who you saw me with at Roscoe's that one night," she mumbled.

"Why the fuck is he calling you at 3 in the fucking morning?"

"I don't fucking know Kyrie, you answered the fucking phone," She snapped, getting out the bed and walking into the bathroom.

When she came out the bathroom, I wanted to snap on her ass, but I just left it alone as she climbed back in bed and pulled the cover over her head. I knew she was hiding something, but I just let it go and laid back down.

Chapter Seventeen
Taylor

"Tay, can you ride with me?" Ty'Shuan asked me as he walked in my room, where I was reading *'Macio & Jalisa; Another Hood Love Story 2,'* by Sierra Nicole.

"Ride where Ty'Shuan? This book is getting so good," I told him as I looked up from my Kindle to look at him. He was standing there looking good as hell, wearing a black T-shirt, some black pants, and the Jordan Oreos.

"Ty'Shuan Jr is being released from the hospital, I want to go grab him and Ty'Nessa; you can always bring your Kindle with you."

"Okay, give me a few minutes to get dressed.

After I was dressed, I grabbed my Kindle and headed out the door. When I got in Ty'Shuan's car where he was waiting for me, he was on the phone arguing with somebody. As soon as I closed the door, he hung up.

"What's wrong?" I asked him.

"Nothing," he lied.

"Why are you lying to me? Ty'Shuan, tell me what's wrong,-." I said as I grabbed his hand; he looked at me and I knew he was pissed off.

"It's nothing," he said as he started the car up and pulled off.

When we got to Arneisha's house, I stayed in the car while he went in there to get Ty'Nessa. After waiting fifteen minutes for him to come back out, I grabbed the keys from the ignition and got out the car.

As I got closer to Arneisha's house, I heard her and Ty'Shuan arguing.

"I don't know what the fuck you doing all this shit for, Arneisha."

"Because you fucking lied to me Ty'Shuan, you told me that you were gon' leave that bitch and we were gon' be together," she said, and I could tell she was crying.

"You should have known I was fucking lying, you knew I wasn't leaving Taylor for no bitch."

"I don't give a fuck no more, you're not taking my daughter or my son. I'll be damned if I let you and that bitch play house with my fucking babies."

"You worried about the wrong shit. You more worried about me being with somebody else than the well being over your fucking kids. You aren't fit to raise them in this bitch. And I never said anything about Taylor raising them."

"Fuck that bitch, like I said you are not taking my children."

I had heard enough. I went back to the car, went in one of Ty'Shuan's secret compartments, and grabbed his 9. I made sure it was loaded, took it off safety, and walked back towards the house.

Ty'Shuan and Arneisha were still arguing when I got back to the house. I peeped into the house, making sure the baby wasn't near, before pointing the gun at Arneisha's head and pulling the trigger. I watched as her head split open and blood and brain matter went all over Ty'Shuan; he looked up at the door and saw me standing there with the gun in my hand.

"What the fuck did you do that for Taylor?" he asked me as I walked past him and went up the stairs to grab the baby. I didn't grab anything else besides her diaper bag as I walked down the stairs. Ty'Shuan was still standing in the same place he was when I went upstairs.

"Don't just stand there Ty'Shuan, let's get the hell out of here," I told him as I put Ty'Nessa in her car seat and walked out the door. I was glad when I turned around and saw Ty'Shuan walking right behind me.

The ride back to Ty'Shuan's house was a quiet one. I was glad his ass was still in shock and didn't tell me nothing, because the way he was acting right now had me questioning if he had feelings for the bitch.

When we got to his house, he got out the car with out even turning it off. I knew he wanted to hurry up and clean the blood off of him and burn the clothes, so I turned the car off, got the keys from the ignition, and grabbed Ty'Nessa from the back seat before walking in the house.

An hour later, Ty'Shuan walked downstairs with a somber look on his face.

"Did you have any feelings for the bitch?" I asked him as I fed Ty'Nessa her bottle.

"No I didn't have feelings for her, Taylor. But still don't mean that I'm not upset that she's dead," he snapped.

Did this motherfucker just snap on me

though?

"You know what Ty'Shuan, take me home," I said as I got up to place Ty'Nessa in his arms, then walked out the door and got in the car.

Thirty minutes later, I was still in the car reading when Ty'Shuan walked outside with Ty'Nessa in her car seat. He put her in the car, before getting in himself.

"If you don't mind, I'm gon' stop at the hospital to get Ty'Shuan Jr," he told me, starting the car up and pulling off.

After picking Ty'Shuan Jr up from the hospital, Ty'Shuan dropped me off at home. I knew he probably wanted me to say I was sorry for killing the bitch, but he knew me better than that. I was not about to say sorry for something I was not sorry for. He knew if the shoe was on the other foot and I got pregnant by another nigga, he would have killed the nigga as soon as he found out.

I got out the car without saying a single word to the nigga and walked into the house. Mea was sitting on the sofa eating some popcorn, and watching Titanic. I sat down on the sofa next to her, and started eating the popcorn with her. I guess she was feeling how I was feeling.

When I woke up a few hours later, I noticed that it was dark, and I was sleeping on the sofa, with the TV on Nick, and I know I didn't fall asleep watching it. I got up from the sofa and walked to my room. When I turned the light on, I almost had a damn heart attack. Ty'Shuan was laying in my bed, and he had the twins in his arms.

I couldn't help but to smile at the sight before me. I knew before the twins came along that Ty'Shuan was gon' be a wonderful father. He always helped Ky out when it came down to the triplets, and now just looking at him laying there, I knew he was gon' do any and everything necessary for Ty'Shuan Jr and Ty'Nessa.

"What are you standing there crying for?" Ty'Shuan asked me. I didn't even know I was crying until he said something. I wiped my tears away and walked over to my dresser. I grabbed me a big t-shirt, before going into the bathroom.

After I got out the shower, I walked back in my room. Ty'Shuan was still laying down in the same position he was in before I got in, only this time he had the TV on and he was watching it. I was walking to the door when he called my name.

"Come lay down with us."

"No thank you Ty'Shuan, I'll just go lay down on the sofa."

"It wasn't a question Taylor. Now come on."

I turned around and looked at him, before walking over to the bed, and getting in.

Over the next few days, things were pretty stressful between Ty'Shuan and myself, and Ja'Mea and Ky as well. I didn't really know what was going on between those two because Ja'Mea was even shutting me out, and that wasn't even her. I knew something was really bothering her, and I also knew just the thing that would get her mind off whatever it was. Some retail shopping. Hell we both needed it.

"So, are you gon' tell me what's wrong with you?" I asked her as we walked into Victoria's Secret.

"I'm pregnant!" she blurted out, making me stop in my tracks. When she realized I wasn't walking with her anymore, she stopped and looked at me.

"When the hell did you find this shit out?"
I asked her once I started walking again.

"The other day, and I honestly don't know
what to do. There's just so much going on right
now, and I know now is not the time to be
bringing a child into this crazy ass world.
Besides, Kyrie already have Kyrie Jr, Kylan,
Kyria, Kyan and another baby on the one by
Mack's sister." My ass stopped walking again.

"What the hell you mean he got a baby
with Maye?"

"He told me that he was fucking with her
up until he met me, then he told her he couldn't
mess with her anymore and she started running
her mouth about her being pregnant. He said she
even took a test proving that she was pregnant.
But he promised me that it wasn't his, and every
time he fucked her, he would wear a condom."

"So that's why you and him have been
distant between each other?" I asked as we
started walking again.

"Yeah, I mean I don't know how to feel
right now. I mean I accepted Kyrie Jr. Kylan, and
Kyria. Then he came along with Kyan, and I
accepted him. But I'm just not sure if I can stay

around for Maye's baby," she told me as tears welled up in her eyes.

"Well, if he says Maye's baby isn't his, then I believe him. Maye was fucking with Ty'Shuan, Dez, and Toby also. She's just a team ho'," I said, making her laugh.

"Enough about me and my problems, what's going on with you and Shuan?" she asked me as we looked through the racks, trying to figure out what we wanted to get.

"I shot and killed Arneisha," I whispered to her, looking around and making sure nobody was listening, or even in ear shot of our conversation.

"What!?" she asked a lil' too loud, causing people to look around at us. "Sorry, what?" I didn't say anything, I just nodded my head.

"And he's mad at you for doing that? Did he have feelings for her ass or something?"

"I asked him that, and he said no. We haven't talked about why he's really mad, and I don't want to talk about it. I don't see no reason that his ass should be mad,." I told her.

"Crazy ass heffa, of course you don't," she laughed.

"So what about this baby? Are you gon' tell Ky you're pregnant?"

"I don't know, I know if I do tell him then he's gon' want me to keep it and I don't think I'm ready for all that."

"Well, whatever you decide, just know I support you just like you supported me," I told her, and she smiled.

Chapter Eighteen
Jermiah

I couldn't believe this bitch nigga Ky got my girl pregnant, but that's okay, I was gon' kill his ass, then take care of his seed. Have it calling me daddy. I laughed just thinking about it; I was gon' have his seed calling me daddy.

One of my old ho's called me and told me that they saw Ja'Mea and her best friend Taylor walking through the mall. I had the ho² follow them, in hopes that they could lead me to that nigga Ky.

****

"Look, there that nigga Ky go right there," Derrick pointed out as we watched Ky get out his car and walked into the building Ja'Mea walked in earlier.

"What you wanna do?"

"Nothing right now, at least not right now. Come on, let's go back to the crib."

When we got back to Derrick's crib out in Albany, Shayreese and her sister Amber were sitting at the table playing cards. Shayreese was crying again.;

"What the fuck is yo ass over there crying for?" Derrick asked as he walked over there and slapped her ass so hard she fell out the chair. Shit, I thought I was bad at beating bitches, but this nigga had me beat on so many levels.

"Somebody killed my fucking best friend you bastard," Shay said as she got up and started swinging on Derrick. I sat down on the sofa and watched them as they fought.

I couldn't lie, Shay was keeping up with Derrick's ass that was until Derrick punched her in the chest, knocking the wind out her ass. She flew back against the wall, knocking the clock on the floor.

"Now get the fuck up and fix me something to eat," he told her before walking out the kitchen.

The next morning, I woke up and Shayreese was sleeping on the sofa across from the sofa I was sleeping on. I knew whenever she and Derrick would get to fighting and shit, he would always put her ass out the room. His crazy ass even made her sleep outside on the back porch sometimes.

"Why do you want to hurt her?" Shay asked me as I sat up on the sofa; I didn't even know her ass was up.

"Hurt who?" I asked, even though I already knew who she was talking about Ja'Mea.

"Your ex girlfriend, the one that's with Kyrie."

"I don't want to hurt her, I want to get her back. I just want to hurt that bitch ass nigga Ky."

"Why would you want to get her back when you put her through so much shit while you were together? Do you think she'll ever love you the same?"

"What are you getting at Shay? What's your point in telling me this shit?" I asked her. She didn't answer me; instead, she got up and walked up the stairs.

Chapter Nineteen
Shayreese

I was gon' do everything in my power to stop Derrick. He wasn't just trying to kill Kyrie, he was also trying to kill my children. I knew that he had to be stopped when he talked about how he was gon' torture Kyrie Jr and Kylan. No matter what most people thought about me, I loved my kids more than life itself, I just had a fucked up way of showing it.

That's why I wasn't really tripping that they were with Kyrie and Ja'Mea; they needed some love in their lives, because when they were with me, I damn sure didn't give it to them; in fact, I gave them the complete opposite of love. I knew it would have been easier to just kill Derrick before he could get to them, but he had a plan for that. If Derrick was to die, right here and now, his twin brother Mickey still had the go ahead to kill Kyrie, Kyrie Jr, Kylan, and Kyria.

I was getting out the shower when Derrick was walking into the bathroom. He didn't say anything to me, and I damn sure didn't say shit to his ass. My damn chest was still on fire from our fight last night. I don't know why he thought I was some kind of weak bitch that he was gon' keep beating up on; in fact, I was the total opposite. I would fight his ass back, even if I knew I could never beat him.

"Bitch did you sleep next to me last night? I don't fucking think so, yo ass better learn how to speak!" Derrick said before I could walk out the bathroom.

"Good morning Derrick," I spat before walking out the bathroom, and into the room.

I knew his ass was gon' try to start some shit with me this morning, and the last thing I wanted to do was fight with his ass, especially when my body was still hurting from yesterday. I just wanted to get the fuck out of there before he started. I put some clothes on, and hurried out the room before he walked back in there.

"Don't leave out this damn house, we got a mission to handle!" Derrick yelled out to me before I could walk out the room. It was like his ass knew I was planning on leaving the house to get away from his psychotic ass.

Chapter Twenty
Kyrie

I knew something was really going on with Ja'Mea. I knew she was still mad about the whole Maye situation, but she needed to understand that Maye was nothing to me; she wasn't shit but a bitch I fucked from time to time. Ja'Mea was the one I wanted to be with; she was the one I wanted to marry I saw nobody in my future but her ass.

"Lil' ma, come here," I called out to Ja'Mea as she was in the kitchen cooking her something to eat. Her ass had been eating too much these last few days.

"What?" she snapped as she stood in front of me, with nothing but some boy shorts and a tank top on. Her ass was gaining weight like crazy too. I licked my lips just looking at her thick ass standing there, and she looked even sexier with the attitude she was trying to have with me. I got up and grabbed her hand, leading her over to the kitchen table. I lifted her up and sat her down on it, and stood between her legs.

"What do you want? My food is gon' burn," she told me.

"Stay here," I told her as I turned around and walked into to the kitchen. I turned the stove off, then walked back into the dining room, where Ja'Mea was still waiting.

"You still mad at me?" I asked as I started kissing on her neck. She couldn't do nothing but moan as I moved her boy shorts to the side and inserted a finger inside her. She let out a moan and leaned her head on my shoulder as I started slowly finger fucking her.

She was moving her hips along with the rhythm of my finger. I licked my lips as I removed my finger and licked her juices off. She looked at me like she wanted to kill me. I started kissing her before she could run her mouth. I pulled my pants down and entered in her with one thrust; of course, she let out a moan as I started stroking inside of her. It took her a minute, to get used to my size before she started matching me thrust for thrust.

"Shit lil' ma," I growled; her pussy was so damn tight that I had to bite my lip so I wouldn't bust early.

"Kyrrriiiee, babbby I'm aboutttt to cum," she yelled out as she dug her nails in my shoulder and started shaking uncontrollably.

"Make it rain for daddy," I said, and she did just that; she came long and hard. Her juices were dripping down my balls and going down my leg.

—"I'm about to cum to lil' ma," I said as I exploded inside her.

Fifteen minutes later, both of us were getting out the shower.

"Lil ma, you pregnant?" I asked her; I don't know what made me ask her that, though.

"No," she told me. I knew she was lying, but I wasn't gon' call her out on it just yet. I got dressed and then walked downstairs, where Ja'Mea's ass was eating yet again. Yeah, her ass was pregnant.

I was getting in my car, just as my phone rung. I looked at the screen and saw that it was Shay.

"What the fuck you want bitch? Matter of fact, where the fuck you at?" I asked into the phone.

"Don't worry sweetie, I was just calling to

tell you to meet me at my old house," she said, hanging up the phone. I got in my car, and dialed Shuan's number.

"What's popping homie?"

"Aye, you know where Shay old crib at?"

"Yeah, why? What's up?" he asked.

"I need you to meet me there, the bitch just called and told me to meet her there and hung up."

"Ight, I'm en route now," he told me as I hung up the phone.

Now that I'm strugglin' in the business, by any means

Label me greedy, getting' green, by seldom seen

And fuck the world cause I'm cursed, I'm havin' visions

Of leavin' here in a hearse, God can you feel me

Take me away from all the pressure, and all the pain

Show me some happiness again, I'm goin' blind

I spend my time in this cell, ain't livin' well

I know my destiny is hell, where did I fail?
My life in denial, and when I die,
Baptized in eternal fire, I'll shed so many
tears

Tupac's *'So Many Tears'* blared through the speakers as I pulled up in front of Shay's old house. I didn't see Shuan's car out there, but I didn't have time to wait on his ass. I made sure that both my 9's were loaded and off safety before I got out the car and headed towards the house.

When I walked in the house, Shay, Miah, Derrick, and another nigga I remembered being one of the ones that killed my pops was standing around the room. I grabbed my guns and pointed them at Miah and Derrick, but somebody came out from behind the door with a gun pointed at my head.

"Drop the guns," a female voice said; I did as she said and gently put the guns in front of me. Shay walked over to me and bent down and picked them up. I kicked that bitch right in her head, and she fell over. I laughed as I felt the female hit me in my head with the butt of her gun.

"What's good nigga? You not talking all that shit now huh?" Miah's tuff ass said.

"Nigga, it's mighty funny you running yo fucking mouth when I'm fucking yo bitch," I smirked. He walked over to me and hit me in the mouth with the butt of his gun. My mouth started bleeding instantly. "Y'all niggas might as well kill me now, because I swear on my seeds, I'ma murder all of you niggas, and these bitches too," I told them, meaning every word.

"Speaking of yo seeds, you don't gotta worry about the one Ja'Mea carrying, I'ma take real good care of it, and make sure it be calling me daddy," that nigga Miah said. I lunged forward and hit his ass in the mouth before I heard a gunshot, and felt a bullet hit me in my back. I fell down on the ground, and the bitch Shay rolled me over.

"Beg for yo life nigga?" Derrick said as him, Miah, the bitch, and other nigga stood over me.

"Nigga, kill me, I ain't begging for shit," I told them as Miah spit blood out on my face before I felt two bullets hit me in my chest. My whole body felt like it was on fire as everything around me started going black. I could still hear them motherfuckers talking, but couldn't make out the words they were saying before I blacked out.

Chapter Twenty-One
Ja'Mea

I know I should have told Kyrie about the baby, but I still wasn't sure I was gon' keep the baby. I mean, he already had four kids, and a possible. I believed him when he said he didn't fuck Maye raw, but shit the condom could have broke, so until I saw a DNA test, that baby was his.

I was just getting home from work, and all I wanted to do was take a nice warm bath, then get in my bed and get me sleep. That damn sex session I had with Kyrie earlier wore my ass out. I didn't even want to go to work, but I was only working four hours, so I wasn't really tripping about it. Now that I was home, I was gon' sleep the day away, and half of tomorrow since I was off work. After I got out the shower, I put some lotion on and climbed in the bed.

I was sleeping good, until I felt somebody shaking my body. I opened my eyes and Taylor was standing over me, with tears in her eyes. I instantly sat up in the bed.

"What's wrong Tay?" I asked her.

"We need to get to the hospital, and now," she said as she turned around and walked back out the door before I could reply. I hopped out the bed, put on my slippers, grabbed my phone, and walked out the door behind her.

"What's going on Taylor? Why do we need to go to the hospital?" I asked her, but her ass didn't answer me; she just walked out the door, and I followed her.

When we got in the hospital, Shuan, Dez, Toby, and some more niggas I didn't know all were pacing. I looked around for Kyrie and didn't see him. Immediately, I knew we were there for him.

"Shuan, where is Kyrie?" I asked as I ran up to him and grabbed the front of his shirt.

"Mea, I don-" but before he could answer, a doctor walked over to us.

"Ty'Shuan, Kyrie flat lined on the table,

but we were able to bring him back. He's in his recovery room and we can't allow anybody back there to see him right now."

"What about his fiancée? Can she please go back there to see him? –Just for a few seconds," Shuan said; the doctor looked at me and I practically begged him to let me go back there to see him.; I needed him to know I was here with him.

"Alright, but only for five minutes," the doctor said, "Follow me."

When I got in Kyrie's room, I wanted to break down and cry; he was hooked up to all type of machines. Just seeing him like that had me feeling sick as hell. I walked over to the bed and grabbed his hand.

"Don't worry baby, I'm here for you," I squeezed his hand as the tears rapidly fell down my face. "I won't leave your side for nothing, Kyrie. I love you baby."

I sobbed as all the machines started beeping, and nurses ran in the room.

"What's going on?" I panicked as the nurses moved me out the way.;

"Call a code, he's flat lining," one of the

nurses yelled out the room.

"Ma'am, you need to leave out the room please," another nurse said as she pushed me out the room. I stood by the room door as even more nurses ran in.

"He's gone," I heard a nurse say. I tried to get back in the room, but the nurses stopped me. "Ma'am you can't go in there," she said, hugging me as I cried into her shoulder. Whoever did this to my baby was gon' die, and I was putting that on my unborn child.

TO BE CONTINUED

Contact Author
CoCo J.
Facebook:
Coreyiandia
Fluker
Twitter:
_cocokashh
Instagram:
_cocokashh

Text LEOSULLIVAN to 42828 to get a
notification when more from this author
comes out!

Join our mailing list to get a
notification when Leo Sullivan Presents
has another release!
Text LEOSULLIVAN to 22828
to join!
Last release:
Deceit, Heartbreak & Lies by E.
Vonne
Check out our upcoming releases on the
next page!
To submit a manuscript for our review, email us
at leosullivanpresents@gmail.com

Join our mailing list to get a notification for

these upcoming releases!

CPSIA information can be obtained
at www.ICGtesting.com
Printed in the USA
LVOW04s1610271015

459962LV00031B/1195/P